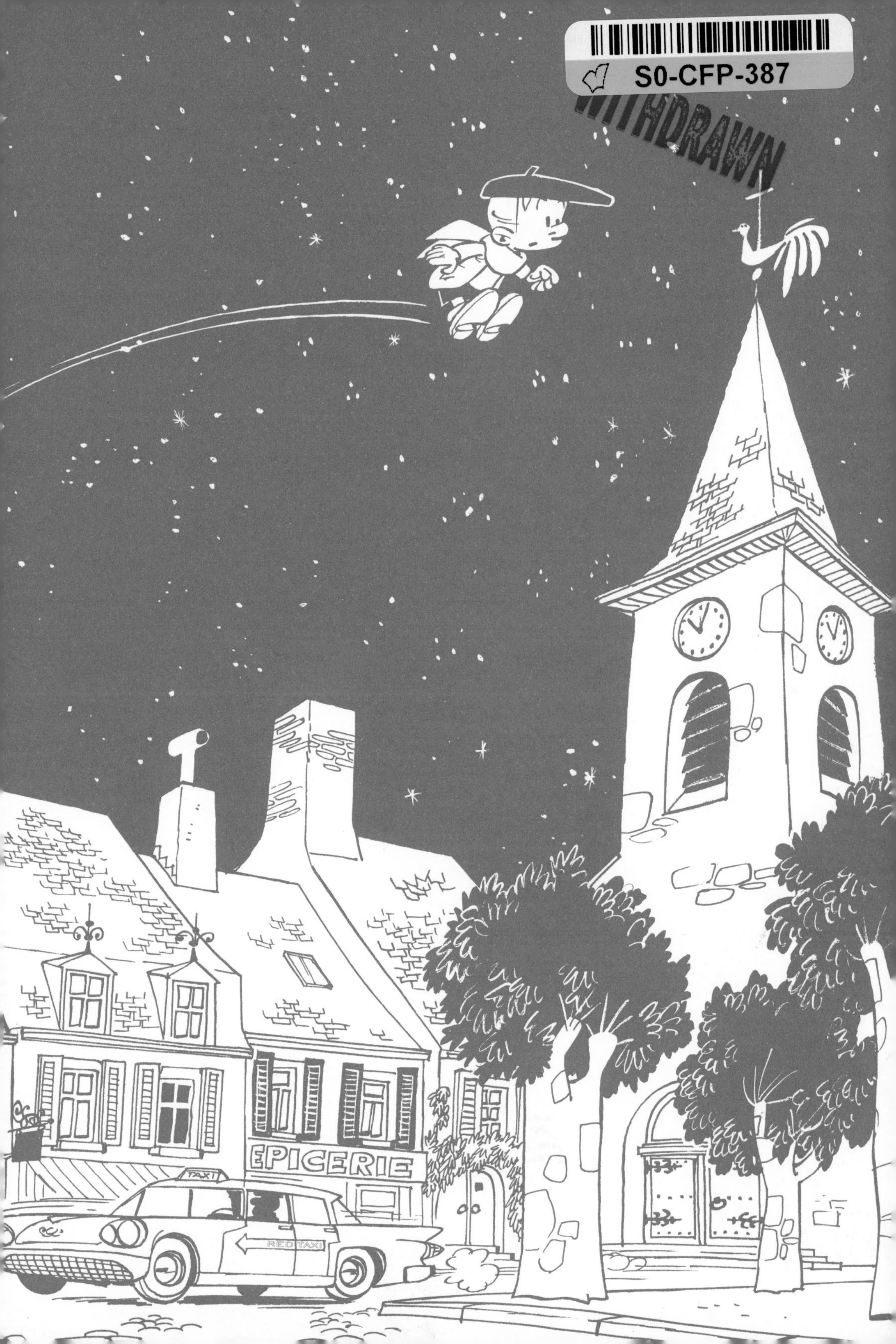
EPICERIE
TAXI
RED TAXI

BENNY BREAKIRON

IN

UNCLE PLACID

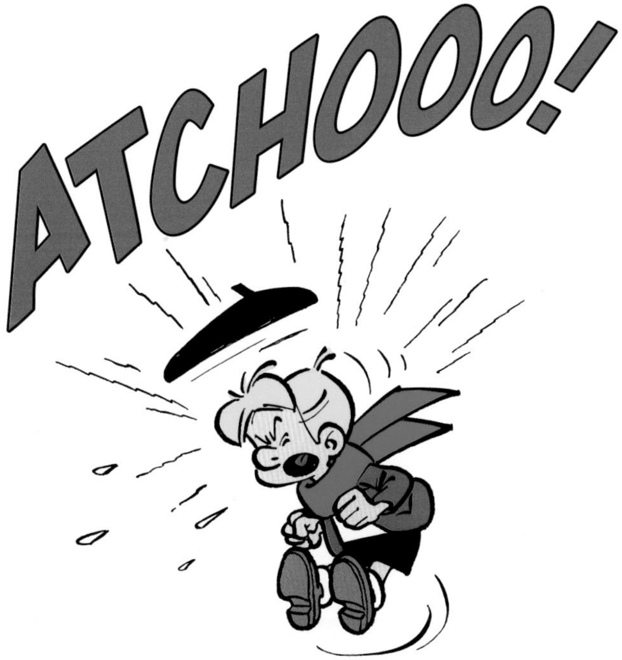
ATCHOOO!

BY

Peyo

AND Gos

WITH BACKGROUNDS BY Walthéry

PAPERCUTZ™

NEW YORK

Peyo GRAPHIC NOVELS AVAILABLE FROM PAPERCUTZ™

BENNY BREAKIRON

RED TAXIS
MADAME ADOLPHINE
TWELVE TRIALS OF BENNY BREAKIRON
UNCLE PLACID
BODONI CIRCUS

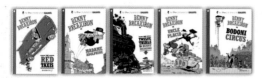

1. **THE RED TAXIS**
2. **MADAME ADOLPHINE**
3. **TWELVE TRIALS OF BENNY BREAKIRON**
4. **UNCLE PLACID**
5. **BODONI CIRCUS** (COMING SOON)

THE SMURFS

1. **THE PURPLE SMURFS**
2. **THE SMURFS AND THE MAGIC FLUTE**
3. **THE SMURF KING**
4. **THE SMURFETTE**
5. **THE SMURFS AND THE EGG**
6. **THE SMURFS AND THE HOWLIBIRD**
7. **THE ASTROSMURF**
8. **THE SMURF APPRENTICE**
9. **GARGAMEL AND THE SMURFS**
10. **THE RETURN OF THE SMURFETTE**
11. **THE SMURF OLYMPICS**
12. **SMURF VS. SMURF**
13. **SMURF SOUP**
14. **THE BABY SMURF**
15. **THE SMURFLINGS**
16. **THE AEROSMURF**
17. **THE STRANGE AWAKENING OF LAZY SMURF**
18. **THE FINANCE SMURF** (COMING SOON)

PURPLE SMURFS
THE SMURFS AND THE MAGIC FLUTE
THE SMURF KING
SMURFETTE
THE SMURFS AND THE EGG
THE SMURFS AND THE HOWLIBIRD
ASTRO SMURF
THE SMURF APPRENTICE
GARGAMEL AND THE SMURFS
THE RETURN OF SMURFETTE
THE SMURF OLYMPICS
SMURF VS. SMURF
SMURF SOUP
THE BABY SMURF
THE SMURFLINGS
THE AEROSMURF
THE STRANGE AWAKENING OF LAZY SMURF
THE FINANCE SMURF

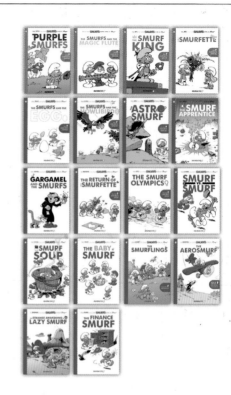

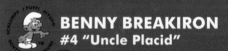

BENNY BREAKIRON graphic novels are available in hardcover only for $11.99 each. THE SMURFS graphic novels are available in paperback for $5.99 each and in hardcover for $10.99 each at booksellers everywhere. You can also order online at www.papercutz.com. Or call 1-800-886-1223, Monday through Friday, 9 – 5 EST. MC, Visa, and AmEx accepted. To order by mail, please add $4.00 for postage and handling for first book ordered, $1.00 for each additional book and make check payable to NBM Publishing. Send to: Papercutz, 160 Broadway, Suite 700, East Wing, New York, NY 10038.

BENNY BREAKIRON and THE SMURFS graphic novels are also available digitally wherever e-books are sold.

PAPERCUTZ.COM

BENNY BREAKIRON
#4 "Uncle Placid"

Joe Johnson, *TRANSLATION*
Adam Grano, *DESIGN AND PRODUCTION*
Janice Chiang, *LETTERING*
Matt. Murray, *SMURF CONSULTANT*
Beth Scorzato, *PRODUCTION COORDINATOR*
Michael Petranek, *ASSOCIATE EDITOR*
Jim Salicrup
EDITOR-IN-CHIEF

ISBN: 978-1-59707-717-0

Papercutz books may be purchased for business or promotional use. For information on bulk purchases please contact Macmillan Corporate and Premium Sales Department at (800) 221-7945 x5442.

PRINTED IN CHINA MAY 2014 BY NEW ERA PRINTING LTD
UNIT C, 8/F, WORLDWIDE CENTRE
123 TUNG CHAU STREET, HONG KONG

DISTRIBUTED BY MACMILLAN
FIRST PAPERCUTZ PRINTING

UNCLE PLACID

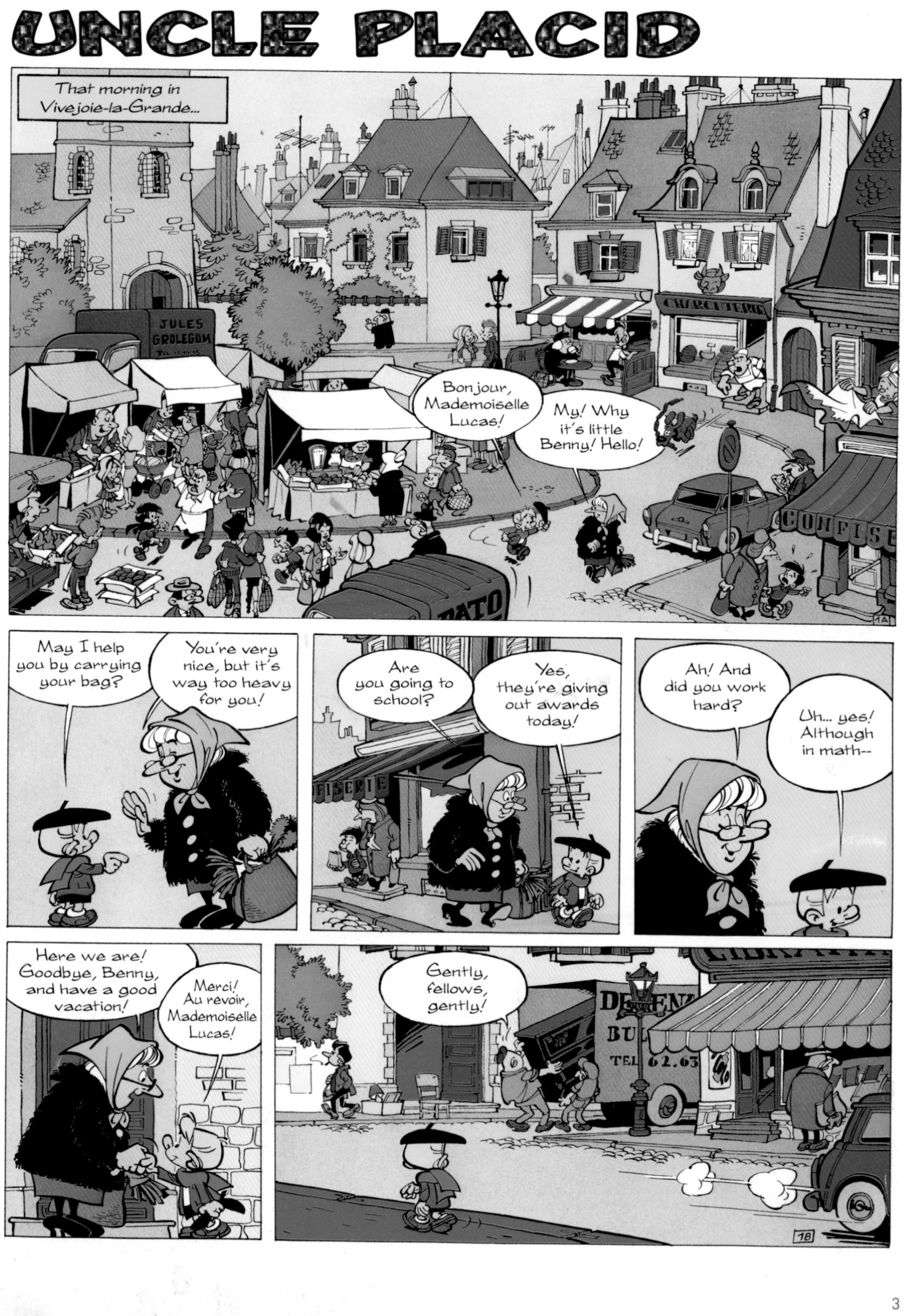
That morning in Vivejoie-la-Grande...
JULES GROLEGUM
CHARCUTERIE
Bonjour, Mademoiselle Lucas!
My! Why it's little Benny! Hello!
May I help you by carrying your bag?
You're very nice, but it's way too heavy for you!
Are you going to school?
Yes, they're giving out awards today!
Ah! And did you work hard?
Uh... yes! Although in math--
Here we are! Goodbye, Benny, and have a good vacation!
Merci! Au revoir, Mademoiselle Lucas!
Gently, fellows, gently!
TEL 62.63

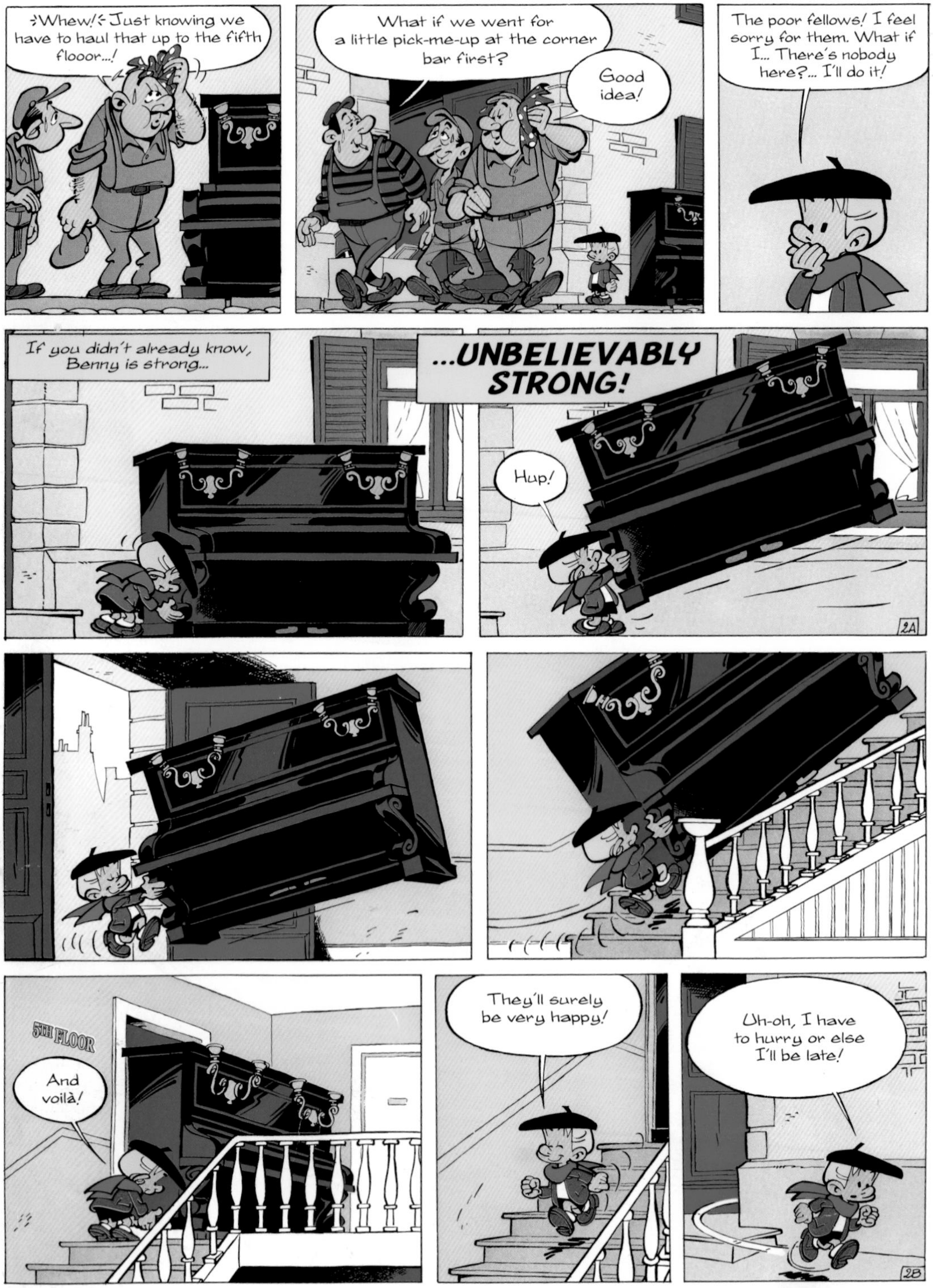
Whew! Just knowing we have to haul that up to the fifth flooor...!
What if we went for a little pick-me-up at the corner bar first?
Good idea!
The poor fellows! I feel sorry for them. What if I... There's nobody here?... I'll do it!
If you didn't already know, Benny is strong...
...UNBELIEVABLY STRONG!
Hup!
2A
5TH FLOOR
And voilà!
They'll surely be very happy!
Uh-oh, I have to hurry or else I'll be late!
2B

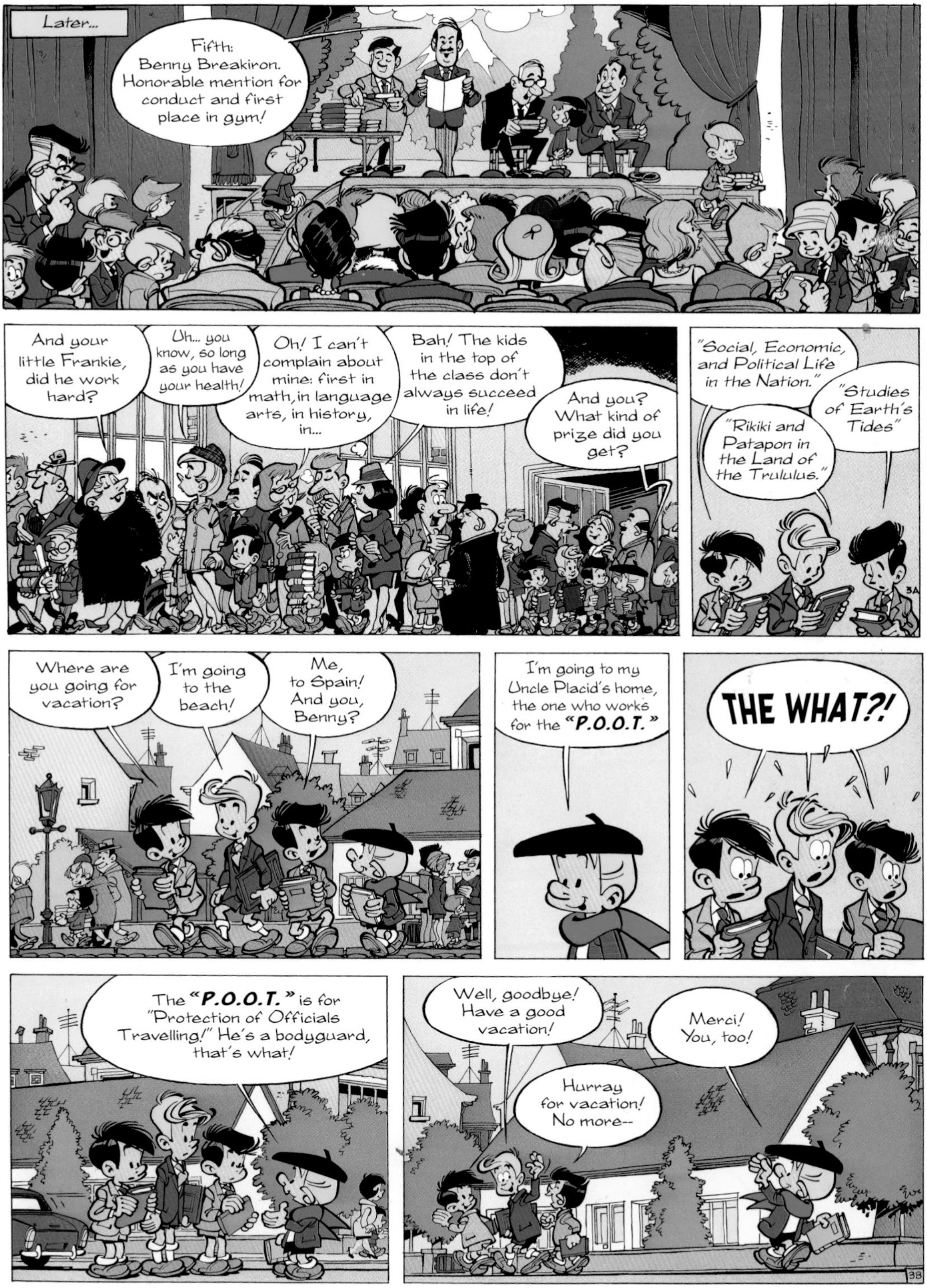
Later...
Fifth: Benny Breakiron. Honorable mention for conduct and first place in gym!
And your little Frankie, did he work hard?
Uh... you know, so long as you have your health!
Oh! I can't complain about mine: first in math, in language arts, in history, in...
Bah! The kids in the top of the class don't always succeed in life!
And you? What kind of prize did you get?
"Social, Economic, and Political Life in the Nation."
"Studies of Earth's Tides"
"Rikiki and Patapon in the Land of the Trululus."
Where are you going for vacation?
I'm going to the beach!
Me, to Spain! And you, Benny?
I'm going to my Uncle Placid's home, the one who works for the "P.O.O.T."
THE WHAT?!
The "P.O.O.T." is for "Protection of Officials Travelling!" He's a bodyguard, that's what!
Well, goodbye! Have a good vacation!
Merci! You, too!
Hurray for vacation! No more--

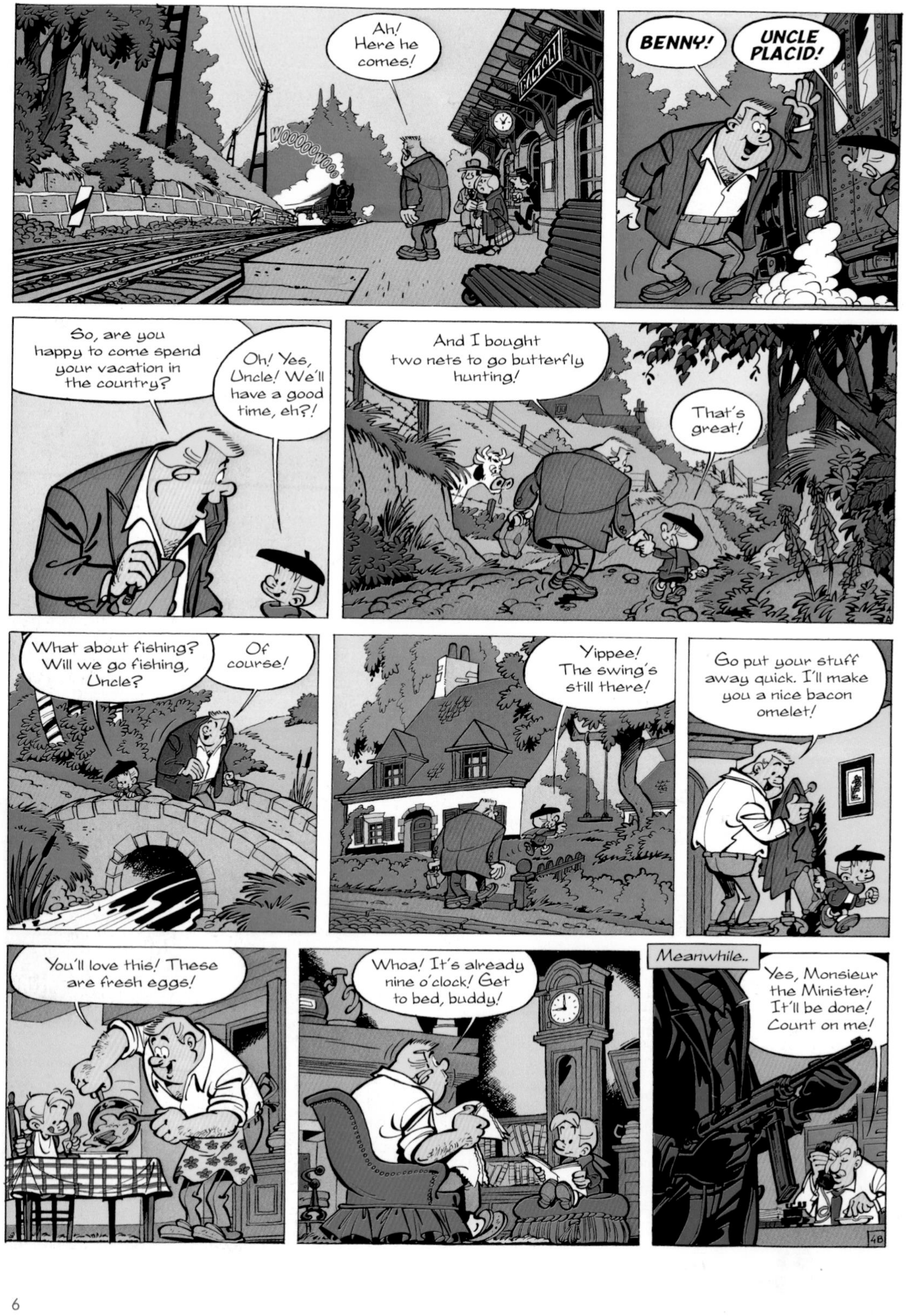
Ah! Here he comes!
BENNY!
UNCLE PLACID!
So, are you happy to come spend your vacation in the country?
Oh! Yes, Uncle! We'll have a good time, eh?!
And I bought two nets to go butterfly hunting!
That's great!
What about fishing? Will we go fishing, Uncle?
Of course!
Yippee! The swing's still there!
Go put your stuff away quick. I'll make you a nice bacon omelet!
You'll love this! These are fresh eggs!
Whoa! It's already nine o'clock! Get to bed, buddy!
Meanwhile..
Yes, Monsieur the Minister! It'll be done! Count on me!

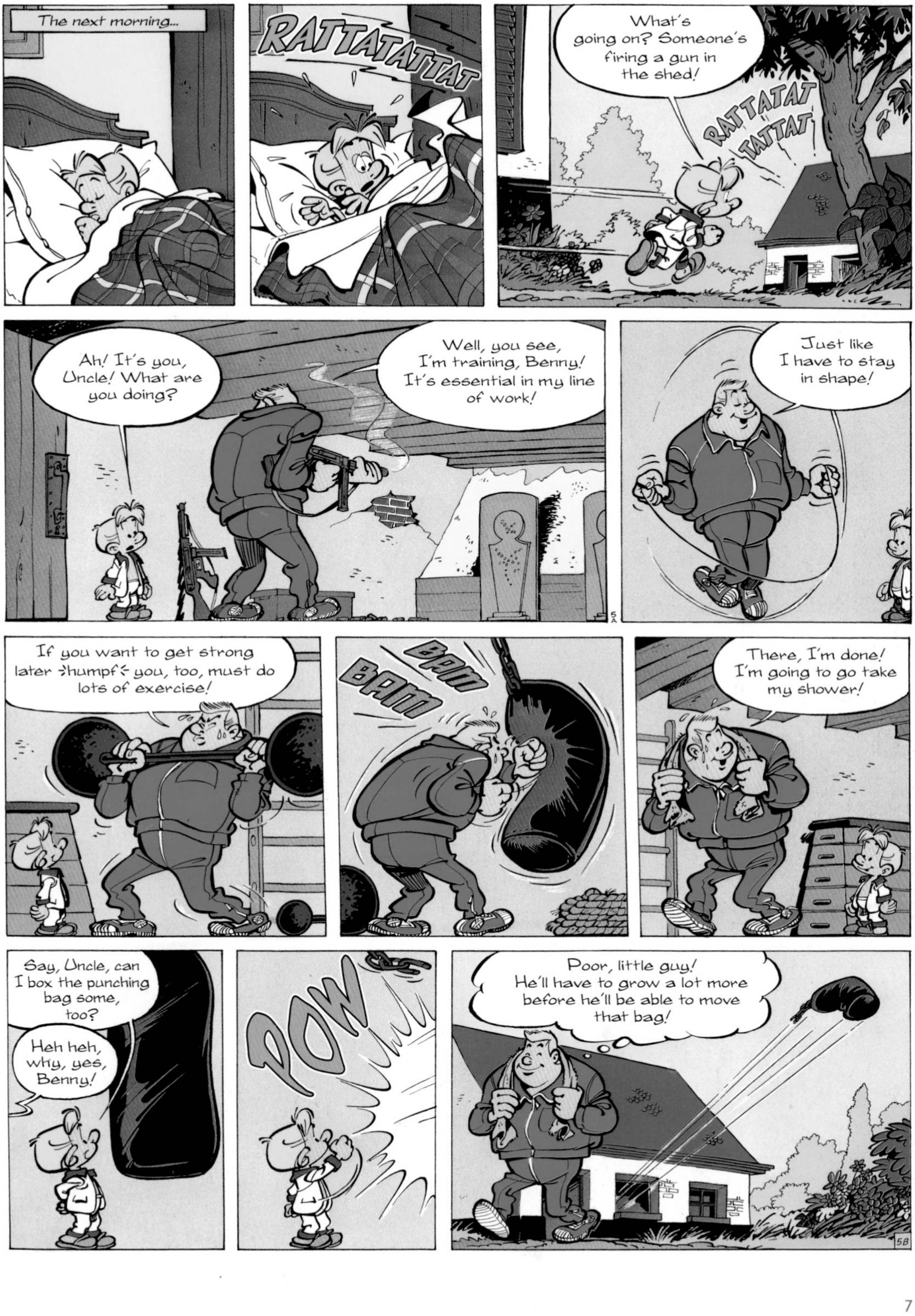

The next morning...
RATTATATTAT
What's going on? Someone's firing a gun in the shed!
RATTATAT TATTAT
Ah! It's you, Uncle! What are you doing?
Well, you see, I'm training, Benny! It's essential in my line of work!
Just like I have to stay in shape!
If you want to get strong later -humpf- you, too, must do lots of exercise!
BAM BAM
There, I'm done! I'm going to go take my shower!
Say, Uncle, can I box the punching bag some, too?
Heh heh, why, yes, Benny!
POW
Poor, little guy! He'll have to grow a lot more before he'll be able to move that bag!

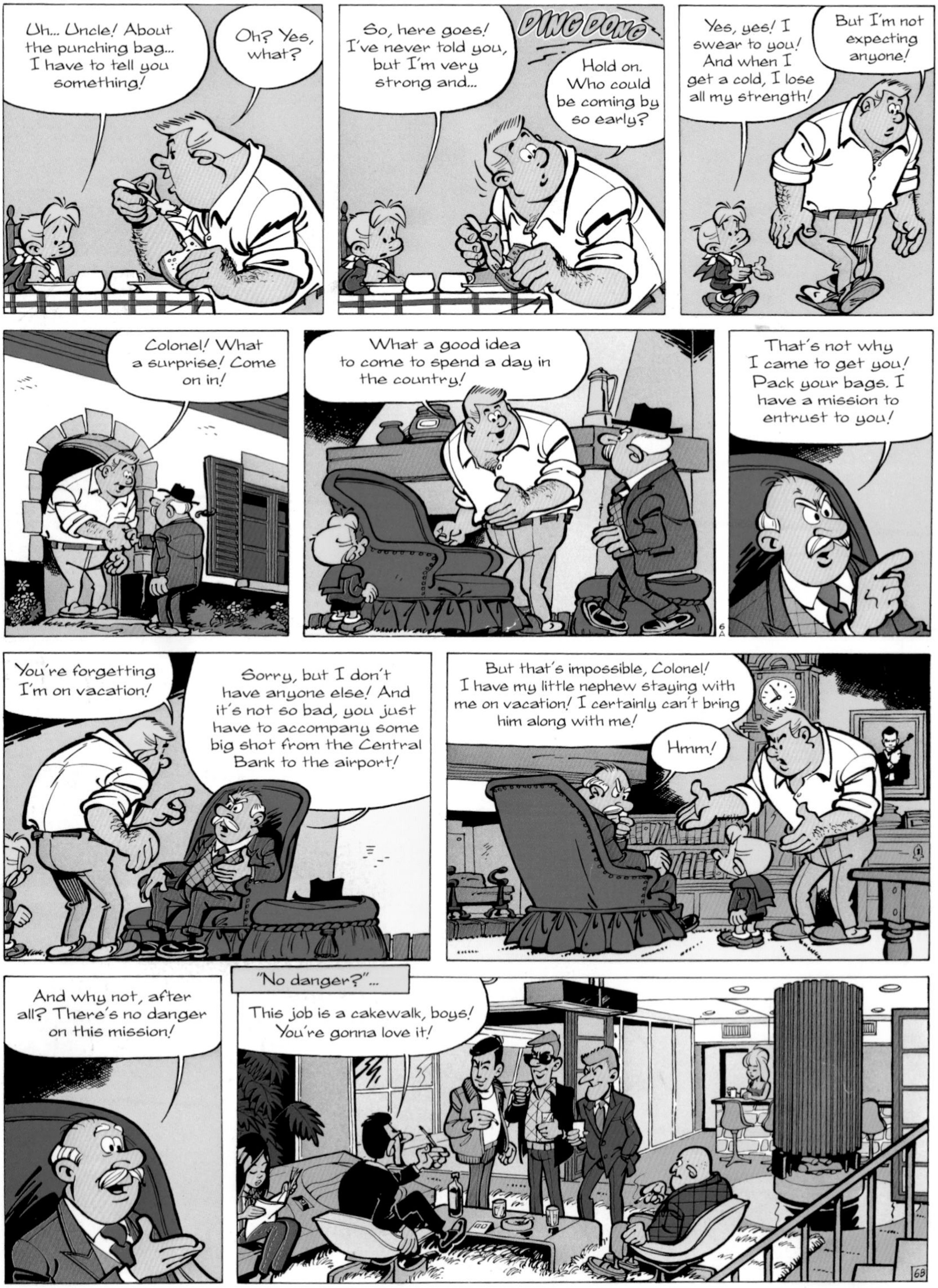
Uh... Uncle! About the punching bag... I have to tell you something!
Oh? Yes, what?
So, here goes! I've never told you, but I'm very strong and...
DING DONG
Hold on. Who could be coming by so early?
Yes, yes! I swear to you! And when I get a cold, I lose all my strength!
But I'm not expecting anyone!
Colonel! What a surprise! Come on in!
What a good idea to come to spend a day in the country!
That's not why I came to get you! Pack your bags. I have a mission to entrust to you!
You're forgetting I'm on vacation!
Sorry, but I don't have anyone else! And it's not so bad, you just have to accompany some big shot from the Central Bank to the airport!
But that's impossible, Colonel! I have my little nephew staying with me on vacation! I certainly can't bring him along with me!
Hmm!
And why not, after all? There's no danger on this mission!
"No danger?"...
This job is a cakewalk, boys! You're gonna love it!

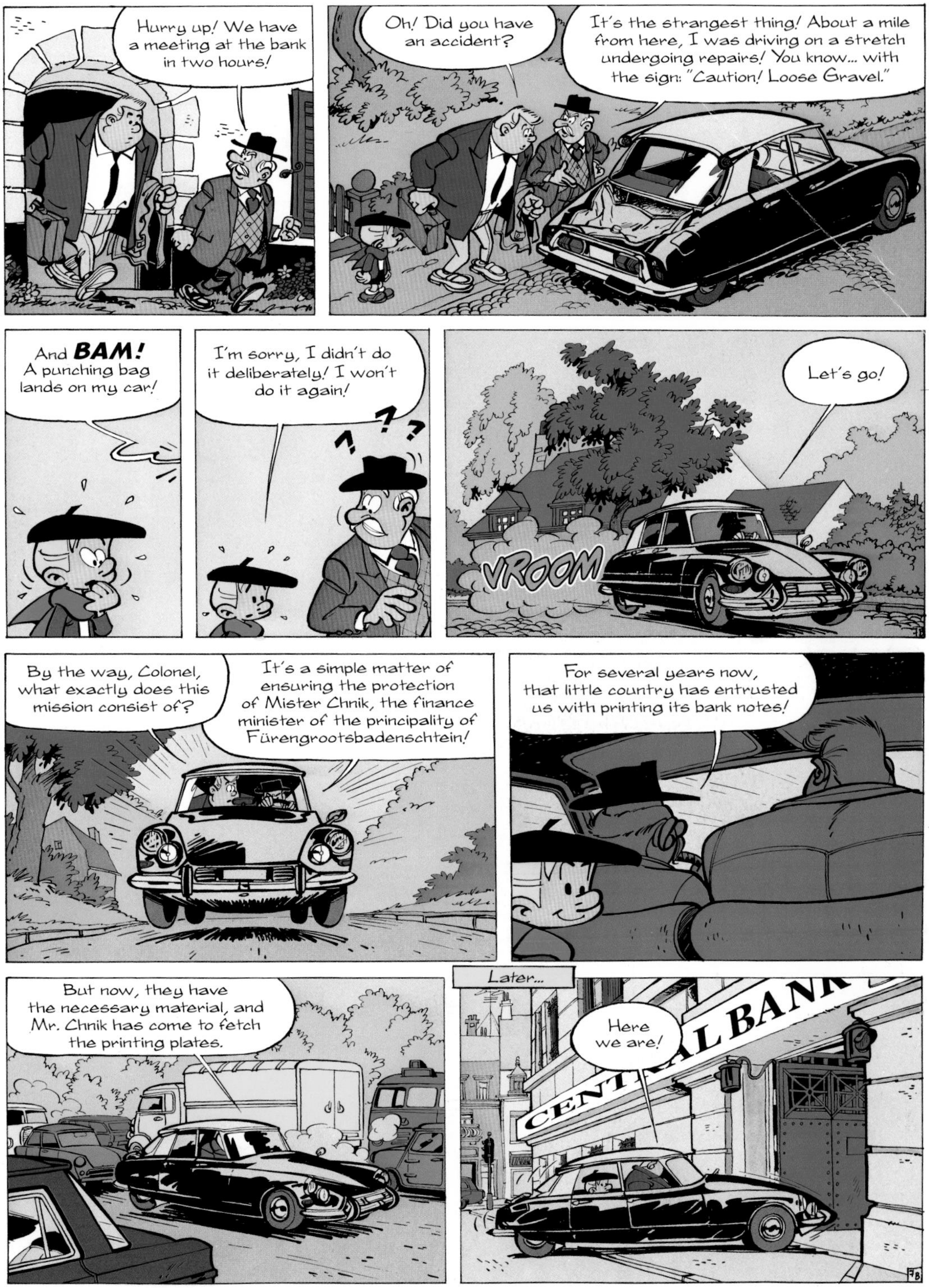
Hurry up! We have a meeting at the bank in two hours!
Oh! Did you have an accident?
It's the strangest thing! About a mile from here, I was driving on a stretch undergoing repairs! You know... with the sign: "Caution! Loose Gravel."
And BAM! A punching bag lands on my car!
I'm sorry, I didn't do it deliberately! I won't do it again!
Let's go!
VROOM
By the way, Colonel, what exactly does this mission consist of?
It's a simple matter of ensuring the protection of Mister Chnik, the finance minister of the principality of Fürengrootsbadenschtein!
For several years now, that little country has entrusted us with printing its bank notes!
But now, they have the necessary material, and Mr. Chnik has come to fetch the printing plates.
Later...
CENTRAL BANK
Here we are!

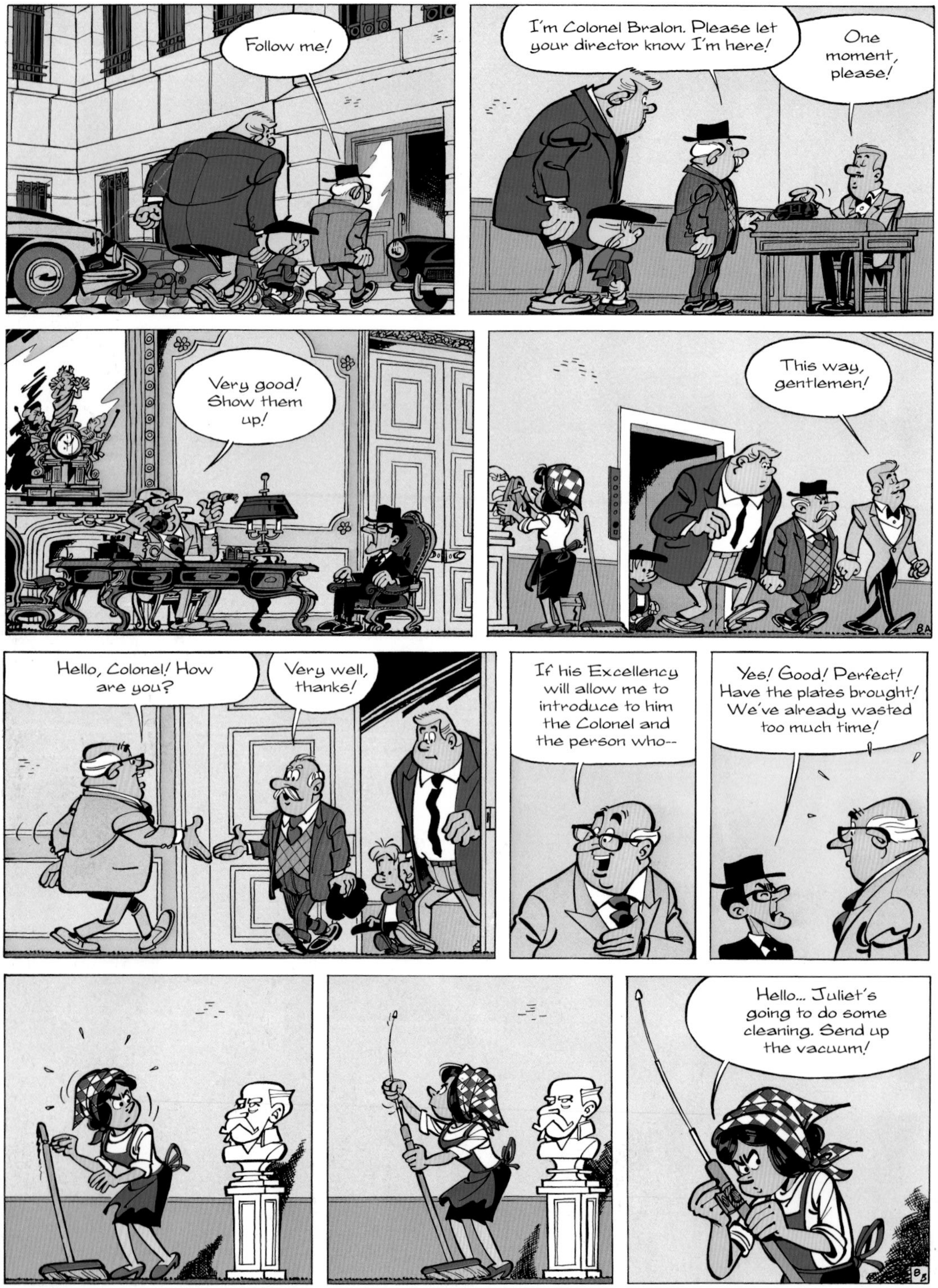
Follow me!
I'm Colonel Bralon. Please let your director know I'm here!
One moment, please!
Very good! Show them up!
This way, gentlemen!
Hello, Colonel! How are you?
Very well, thanks!
If his Excellency will allow me to introduce to him the Colonel and the person who--
Yes! Good! Perfect! Have the plates brought! We've already wasted too much time!
Hello... Juliet's going to do some cleaning. Send up the vacuum!

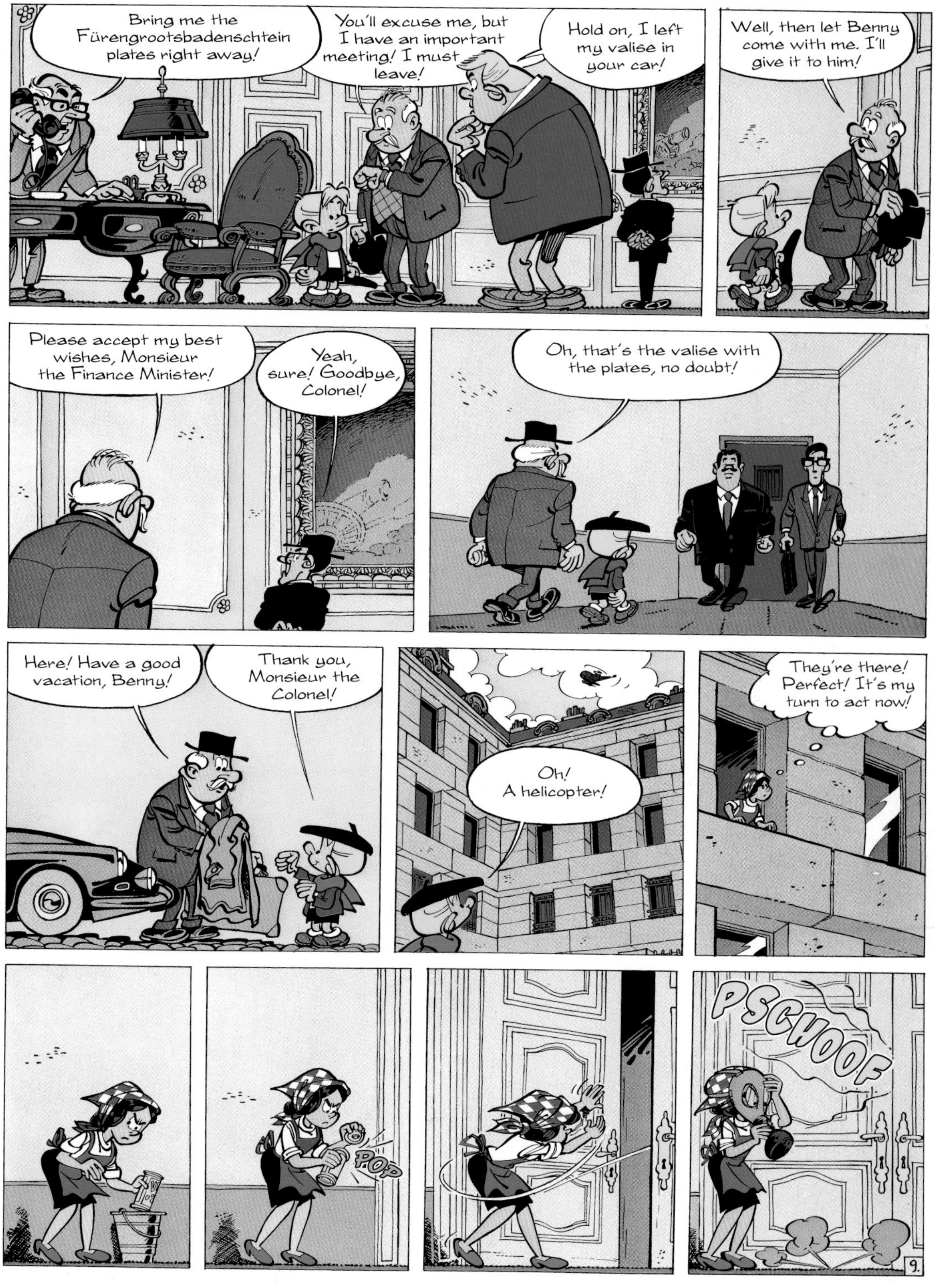
Bring me the Fürengrootsbadenschtein plates right away!
You'll excuse me, but I have an important meeting! I must leave!
Hold on, I left my valise in your car!
Well, then let Benny come with me. I'll give it to him!
Please accept my best wishes, Monsieur the Finance Minister!
Yeah, sure! Goodbye, Colonel!
Oh, that's the valise with the plates, no doubt!
Here! Have a good vacation, Benny!
Thank you, Monsieur the Colonel!
Oh! A helicopter!
They're there! Perfect! It's my turn to act now!
POP
PSCHOOF
9.

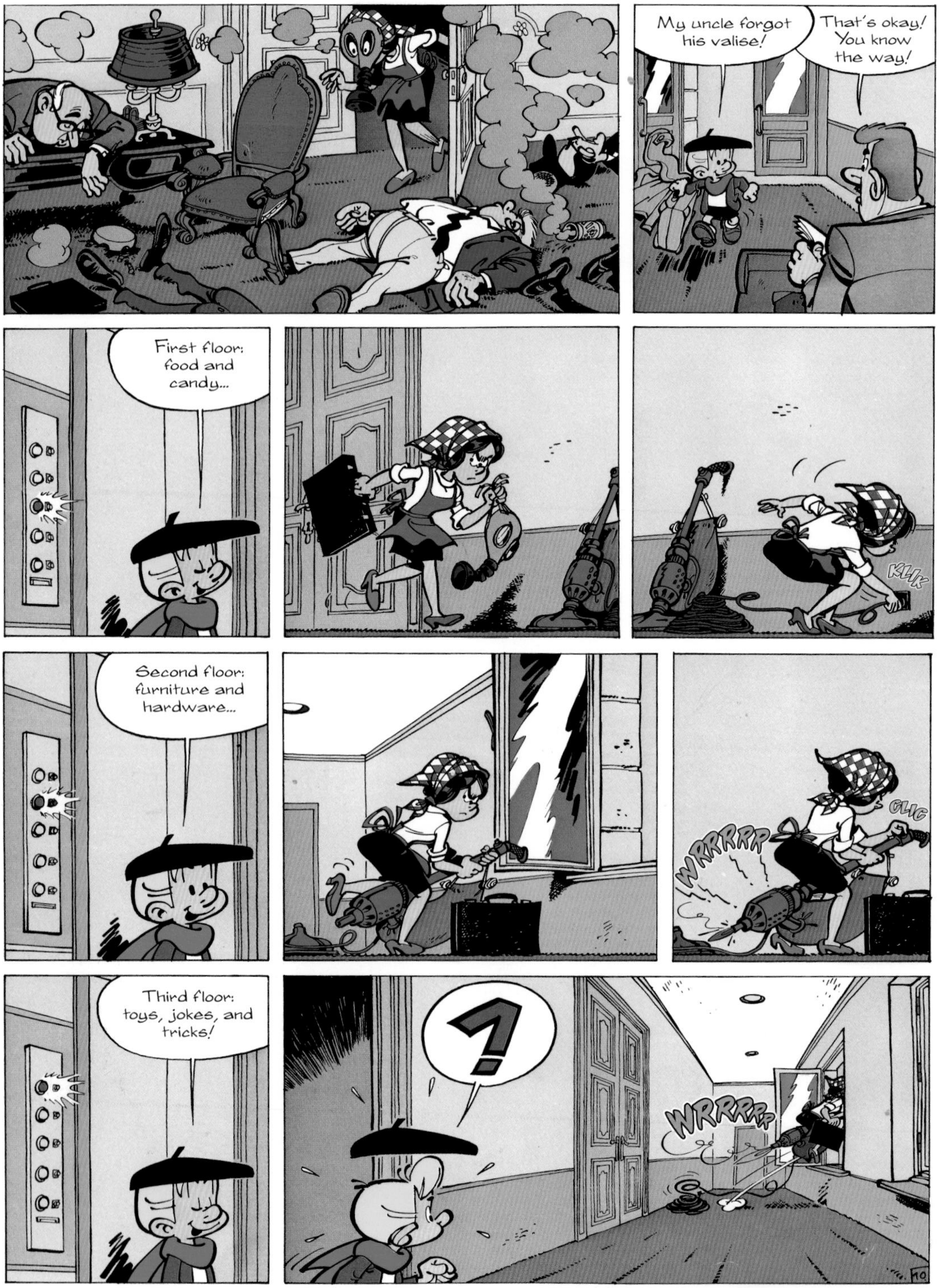
My uncle forgot his valise!
That's okay! You know the way!
First floor: food and candy...
KLIK
Second floor: furniture and hardware...
WRRRRR
CLIC
Third floor: toys, jokes, and tricks!
?
WRRRRR

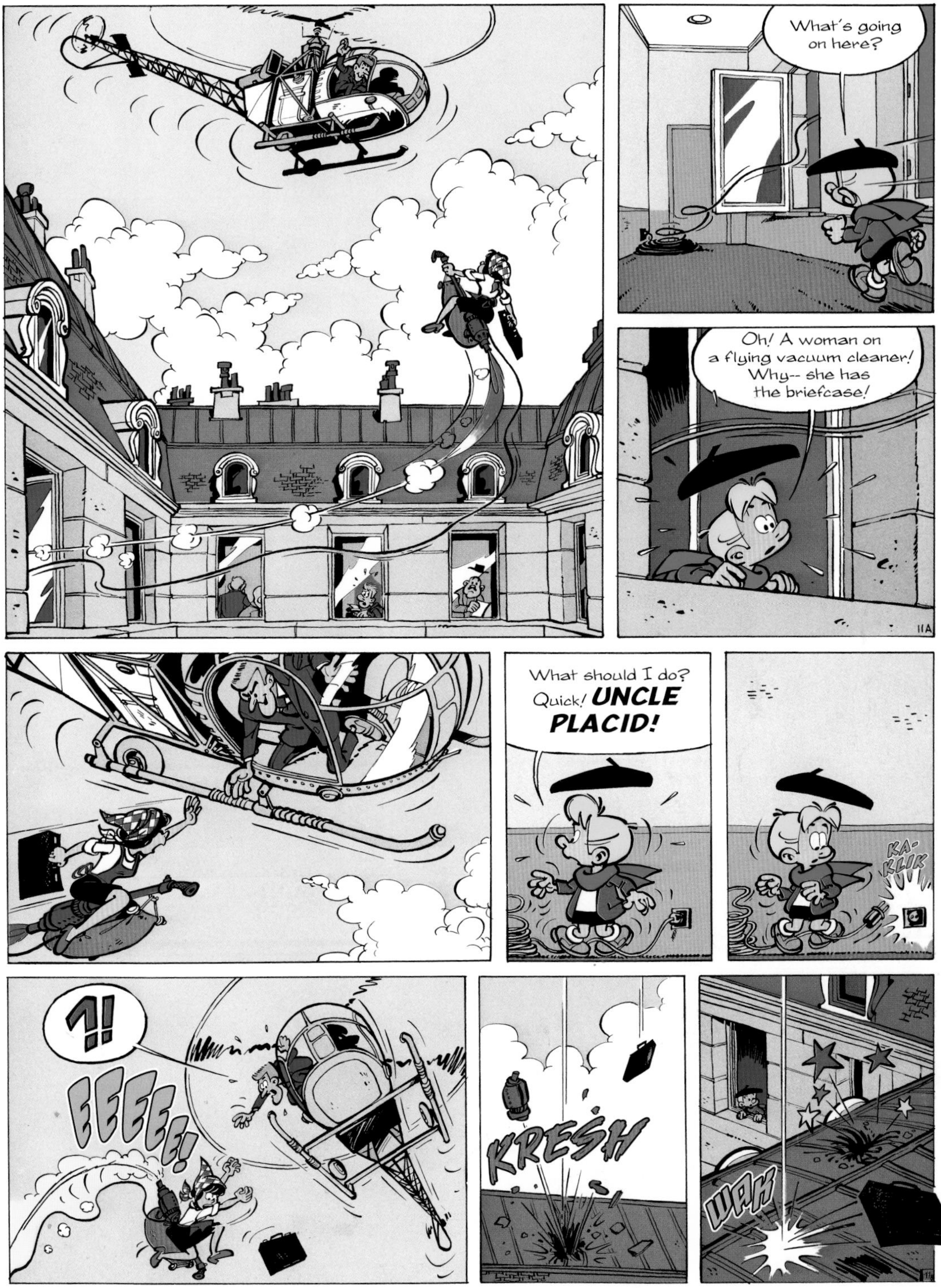
What's going on here?
Oh! A woman on a flying vacuum cleaner! Why-- she has the briefcase!
What should I do? Quick! UNCLE PLACID!
KA-KLIK
?!
EEEEE!
KRESH
WAK

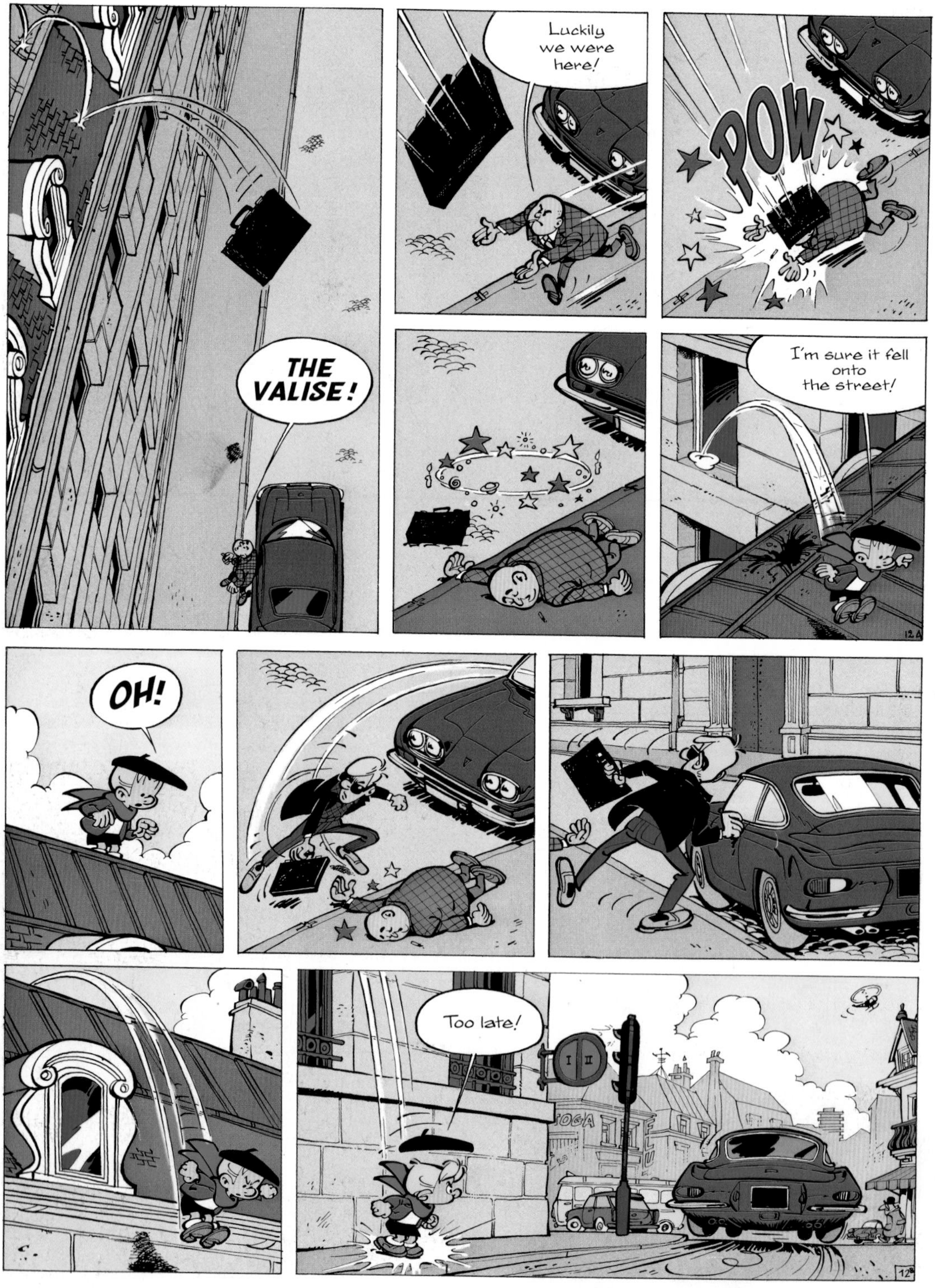
THE VALISE!
Luckily we were here!
POW
I'm sure it fell onto the street!
OH!
Too late!

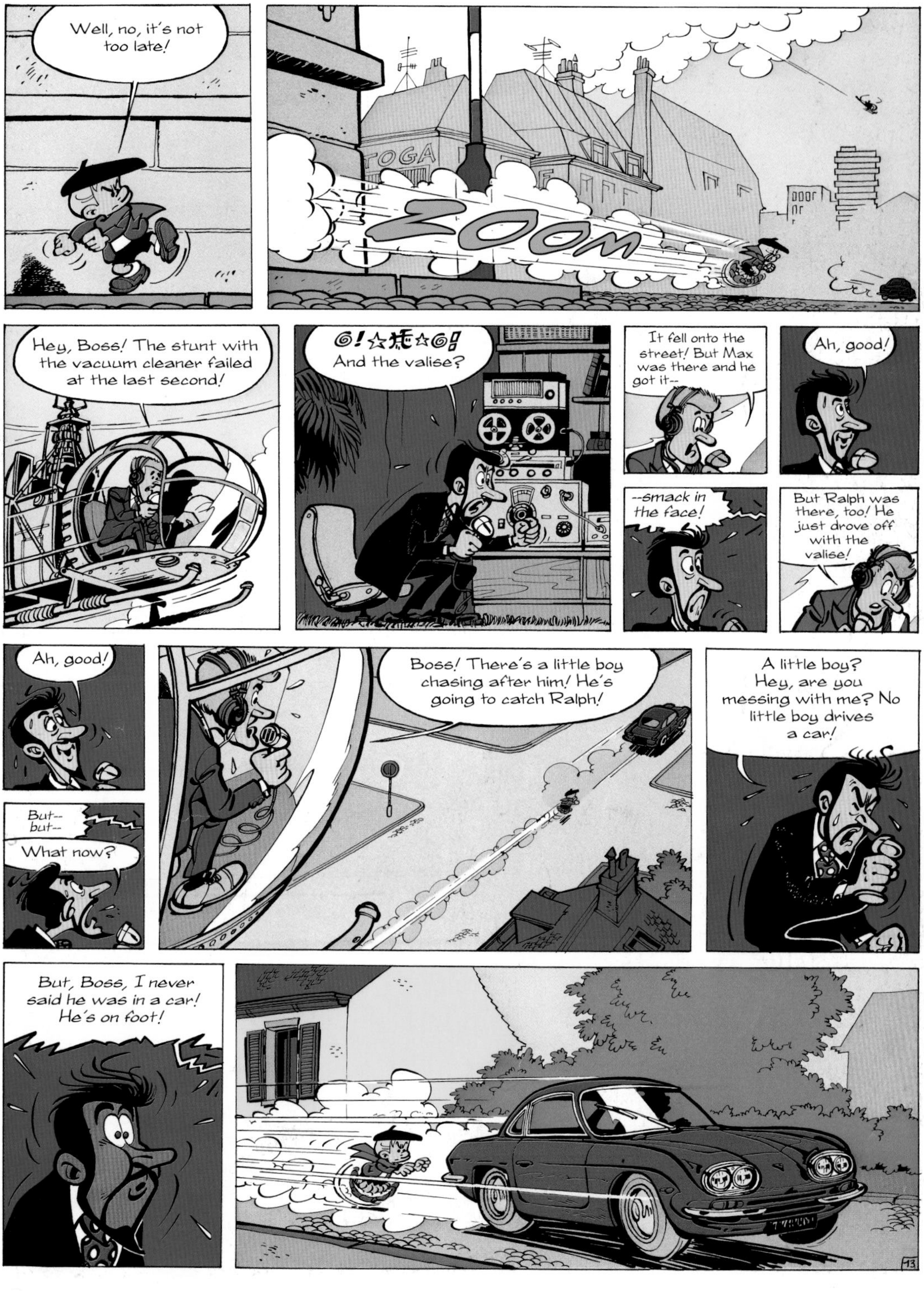
Well, no, it's not too late!
ZOOM
TOGA
Hey, Boss! The stunt with the vacuum cleaner failed at the last second!
And the valise?
It fell onto the street! But Max was there and he got it--
Ah, good!
--smack in the face!
But Ralph was there, too! He just drove off with the valise!
Ah, good!
But-- but--
What now?
Boss! There's a little boy chasing after him! He's going to catch Ralph!
A little boy? Hey, are you messing with me? No little boy drives a car!
But, Boss, I never said he was in a car! He's on foot!
13

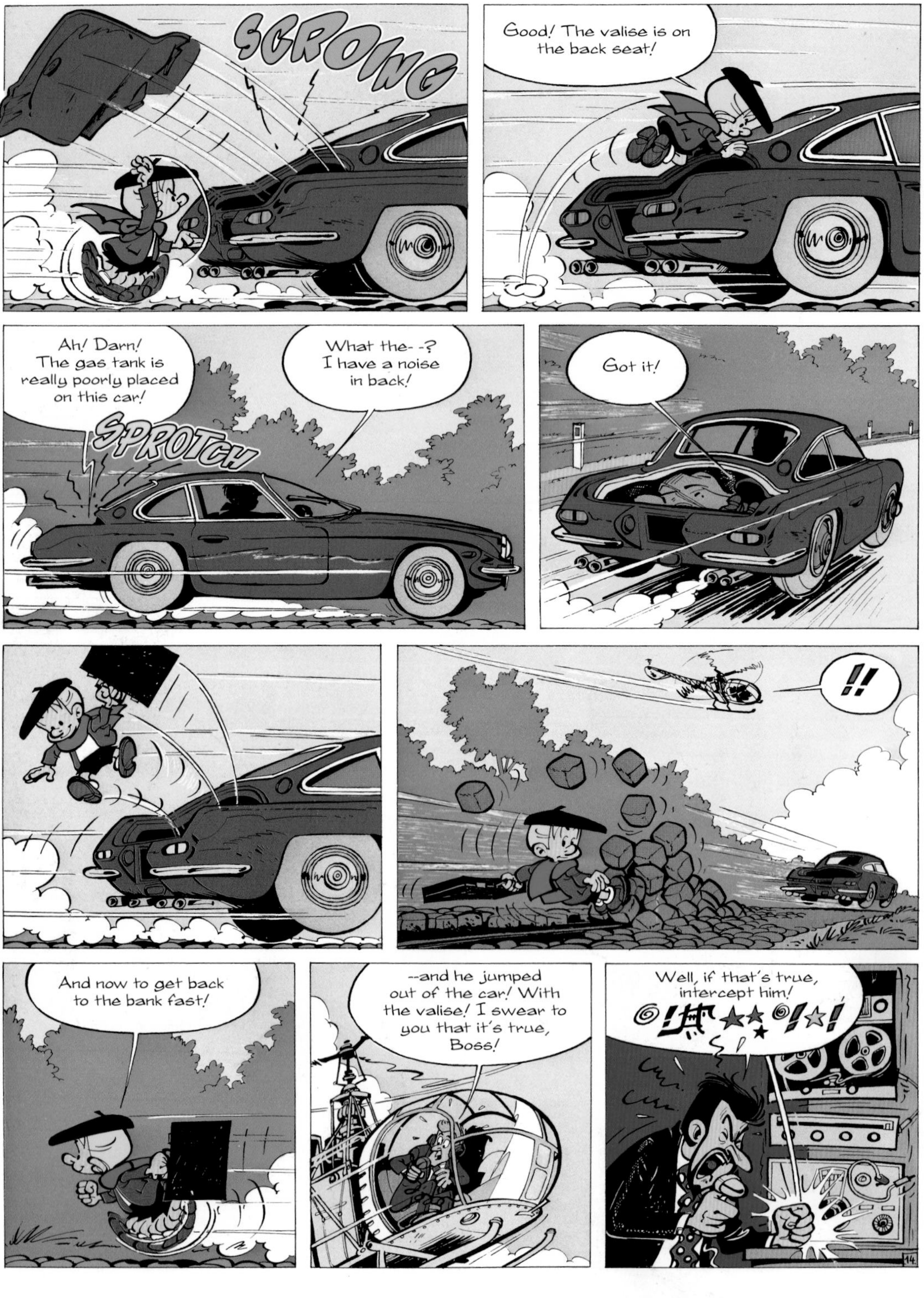
SCROING
Good! The valise is on the back seat!
Ah! Darn! The gas tank is really poorly placed on this car!
SPROTCH
What the--? I have a noise in back!
Got it!
!!
And now to get back to the bank fast!
--and he jumped out of the car! With the valise! I swear to you that it's true, Boss!
Well, if that's true, intercept him!
14

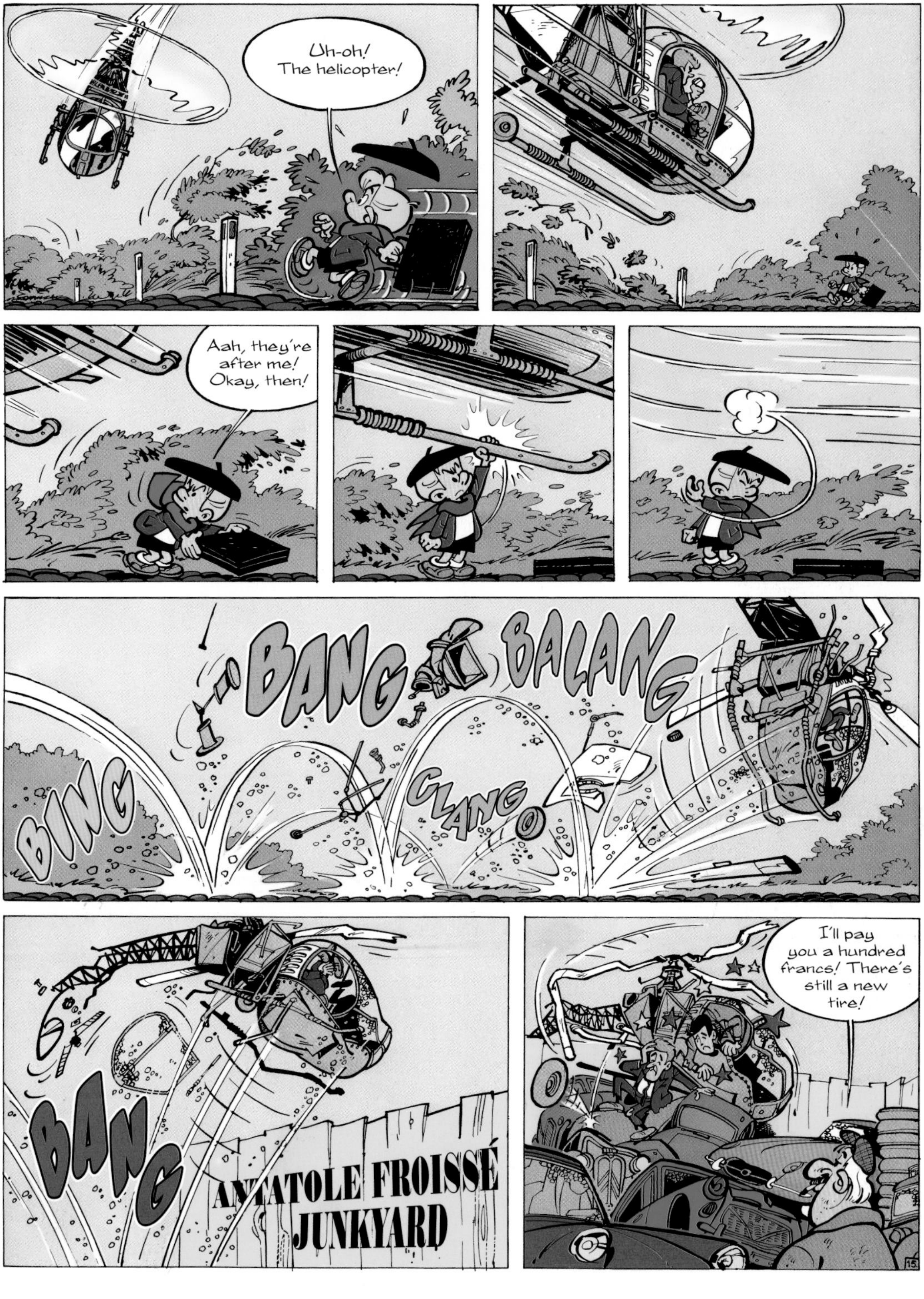
Uh-oh! The helicopter!
Aah, they're after me! Okay, then!
BANG
BALANG
BING
CLANG
BANG
ANATOLE FROISSÉ JUNKYARD
I'll pay you a hundred francs! There's still a new tire!
15

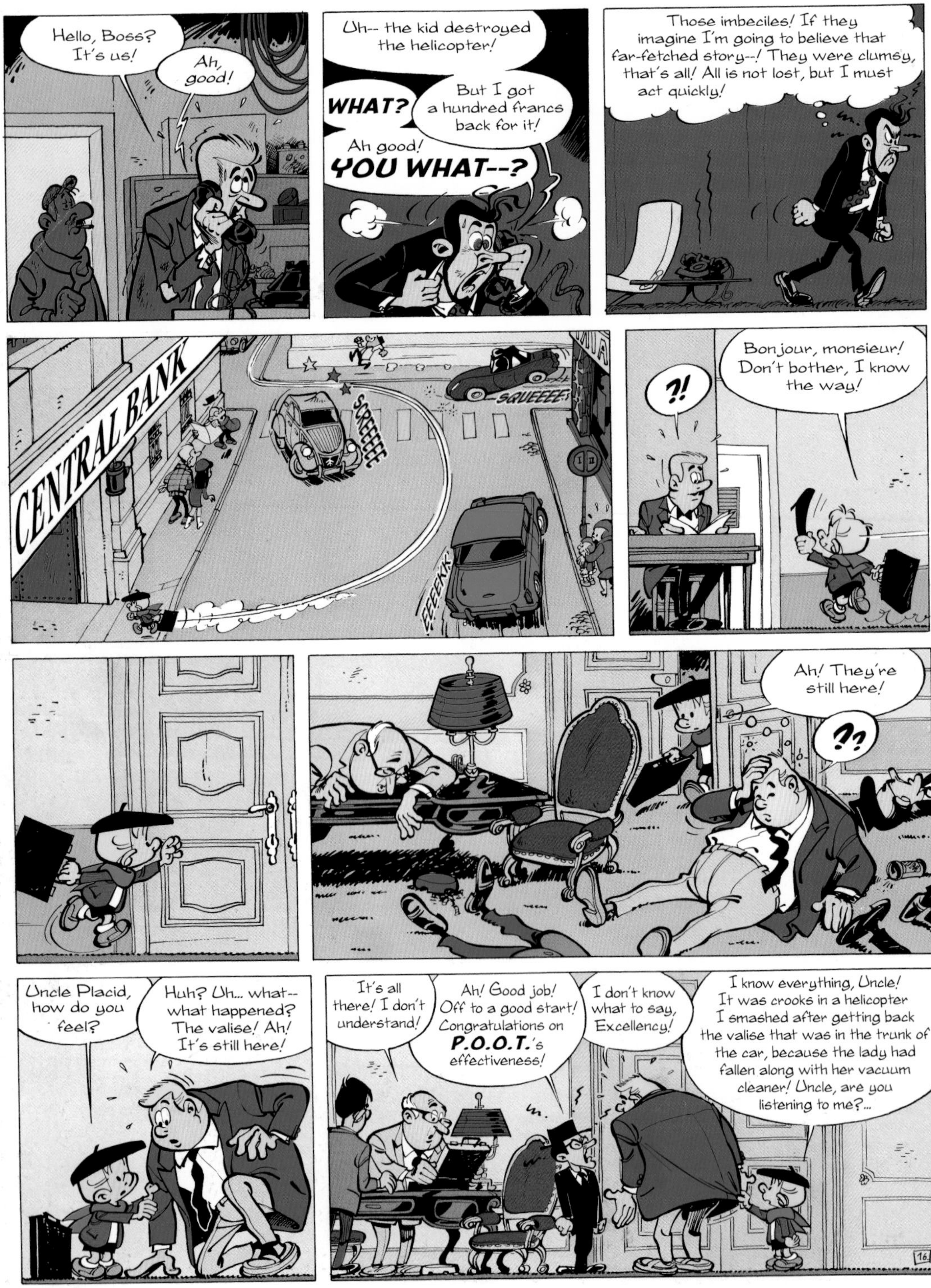
Hello, Boss? It's us!
Ah, good!
Uh-- the kid destroyed the helicopter!
WHAT?
But I got a hundred francs back for it!
Ah good! YOU WHAT--?
Those imbeciles! If they imagine I'm going to believe that far-fetched story--! They were clumsy, that's all! All is not lost, but I must act quickly!
CENTRAL BANK
SCREEEEE
SQUEEEEE
EEEEEKK
?!
Bonjour, monsieur! Don't bother, I know the way!
Ah! They're still here!
??
Uncle Placid, how do you feel?
Huh? Uh... what--what happened? The valise! Ah! It's still here!
It's all there! I don't understand!
Ah! Good job! Off to a good start! Congratulations on P.O.O.T.'s effectiveness!
I don't know what to say, Excellency!
I know everything, Uncle! It was crooks in a helicopter I smashed after getting back the valise that was in the trunk of the car, because the lady had fallen along with her vacuum cleaner! Uncle, are you listening to me?...
16

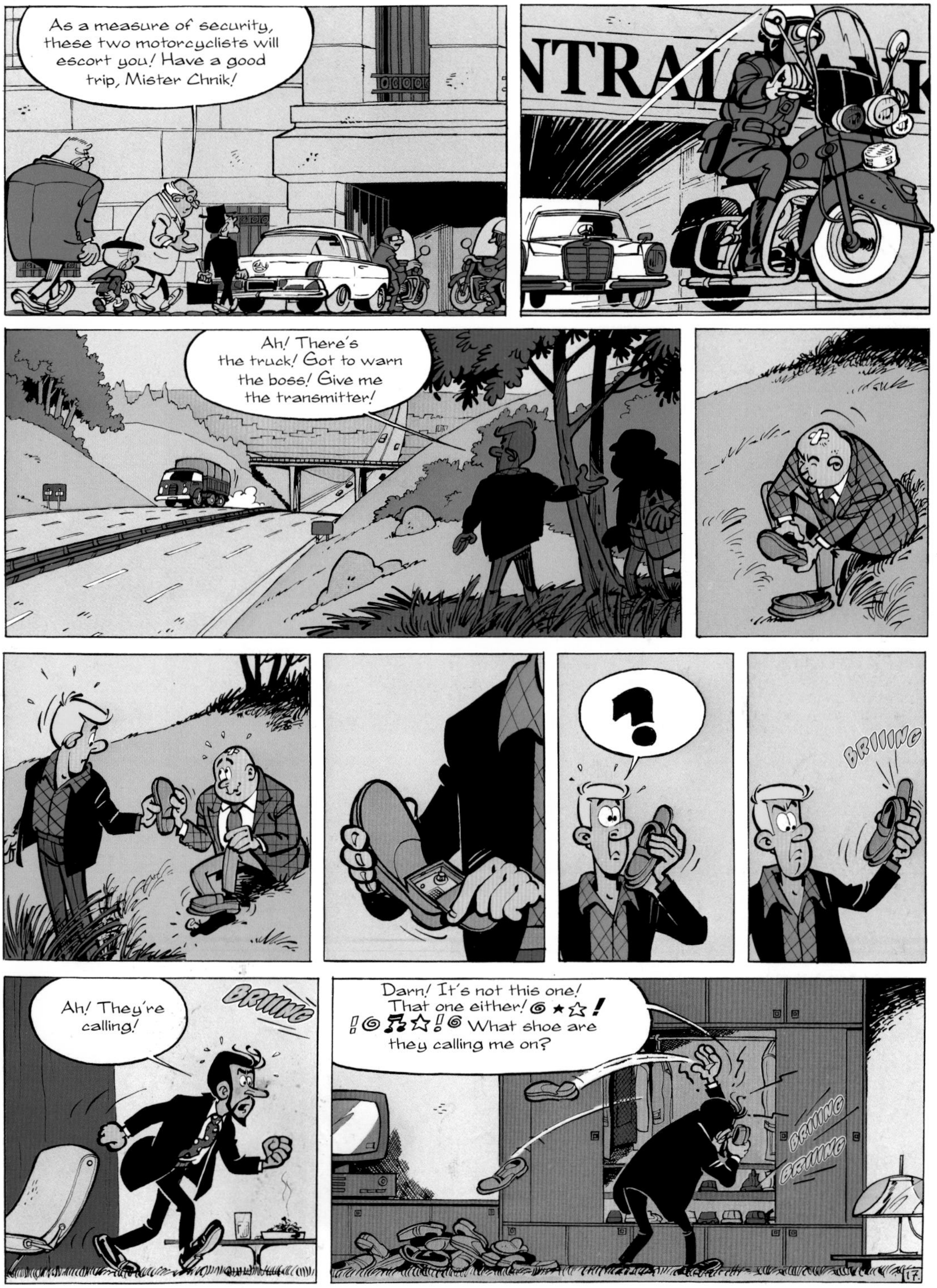

As a measure of security, these two motorcyclists will escort you! Have a good trip, Mister Chnik!
Ah! There's the truck! Got to warn the boss! Give me the transmitter!
?
BRIIING
Ah! They're calling!
BRIIING
Darn! It's not this one! That one either! What shoe are they calling me on?
BRIIING
BRIIING
17.

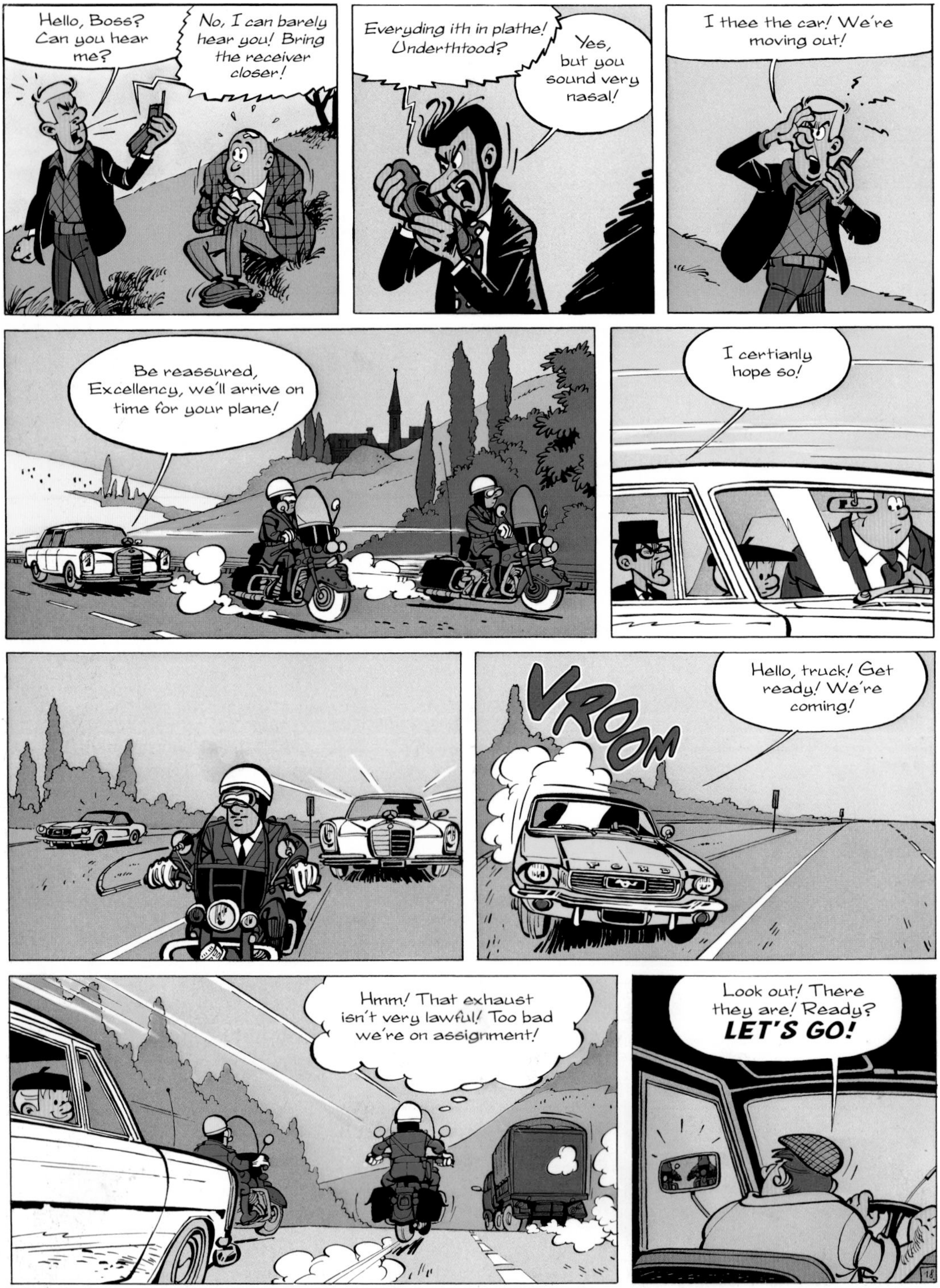
Hello, Boss? Can you hear me?
No, I can barely hear you! Bring the receiver closer!
Everyding ith in plathe! Underthtood?
Yes, but you sound very nasal!
I thee the car! We're moving out!
Be reassured, Excellency, we'll arrive on time for your plane!
I certianly hope so!
VROOM
Hello, truck! Get ready! We're coming!
Hmm! That exhaust isn't very lawful! Too bad we're on assignment!
Look out! There they are! Ready? LET'S GO!

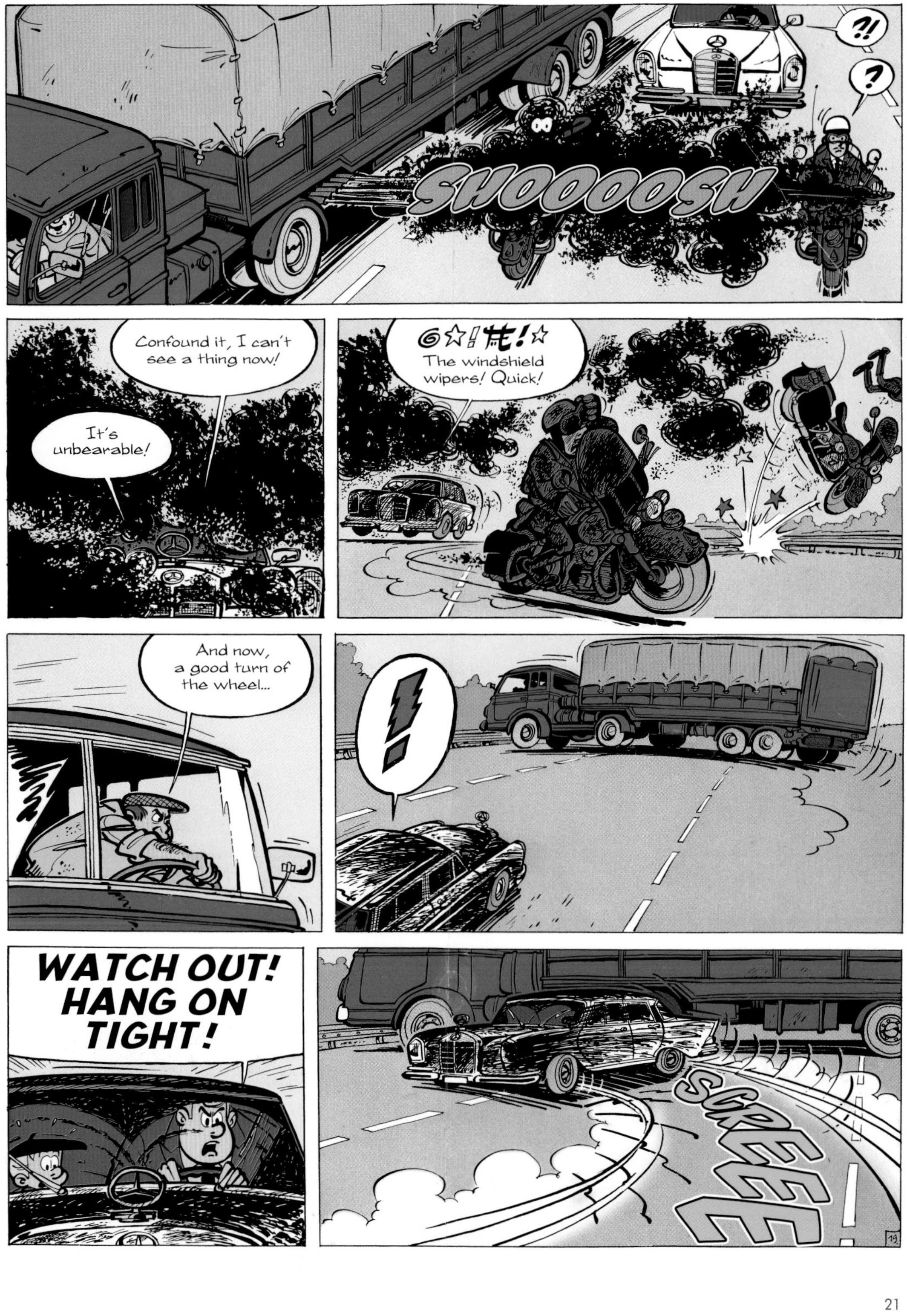

?!!
?
SHOOOOSH
Confound it, I can't see a thing now!
It's unbearable!
The windshield wipers! Quick!
And now, a good turn of the wheel...
!
WATCH OUT! HANG ON TIGHT!
SCREEE!

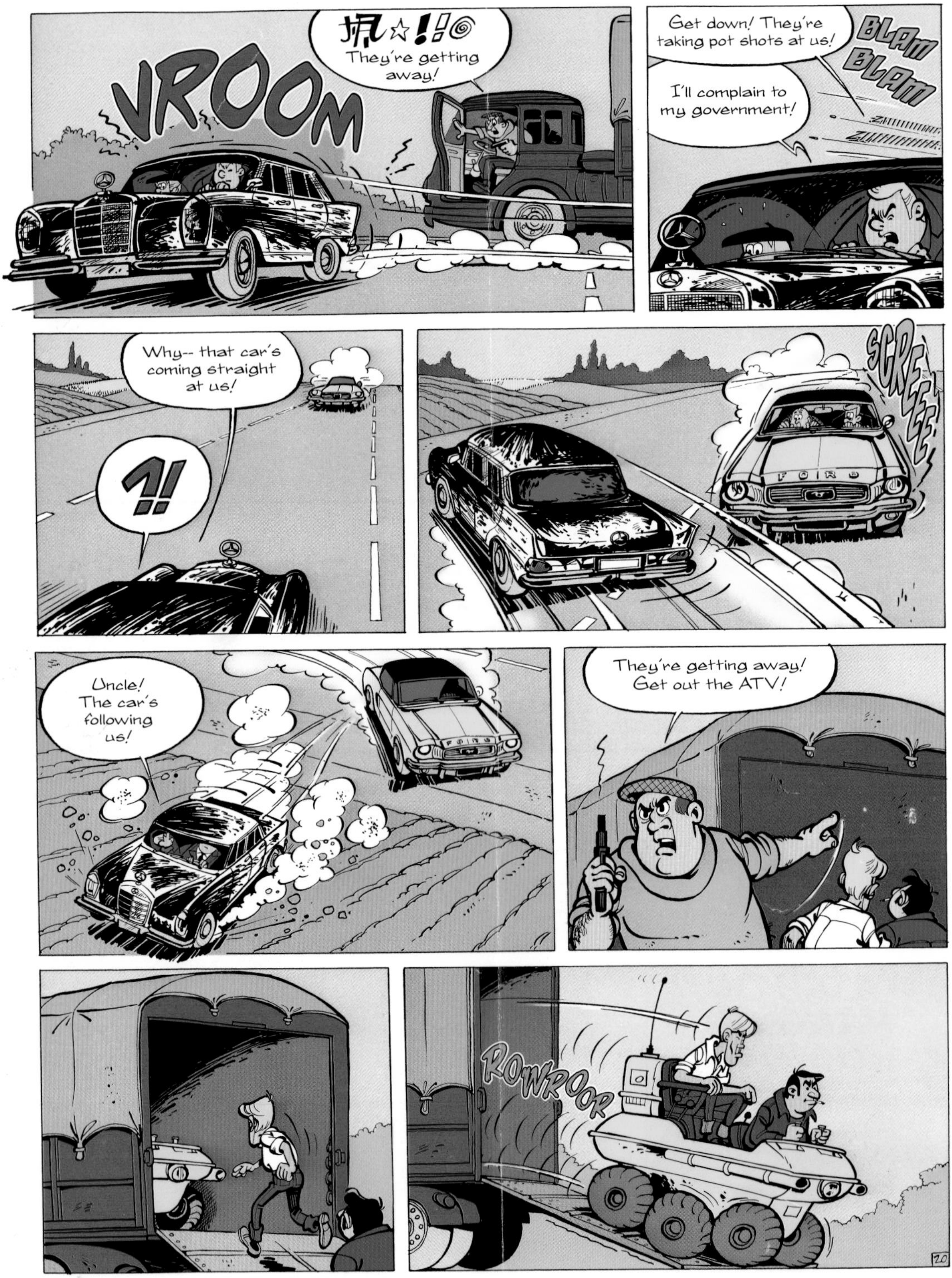
VROOM
They're getting away!
Get down! They're taking pot shots at us!
BLAM
BLAM
I'll complain to my government!
Why-- that car's coming straight at us!
?!!
SCREEE
Uncle! The car's following us!
They're getting away! Get out the ATV!
ROWROOR

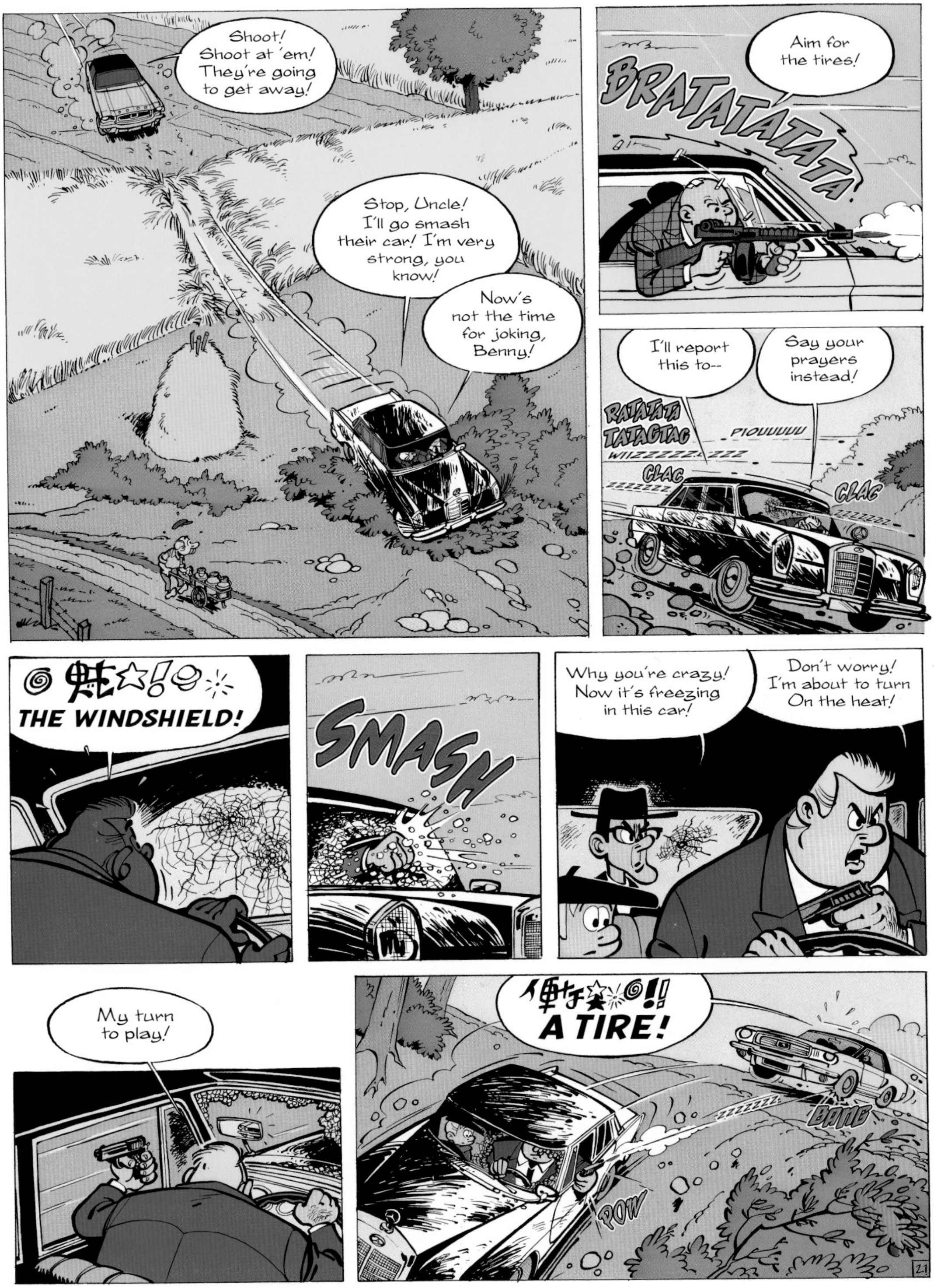

Shoot! Shoot at 'em! They're going to get away!
Stop, Uncle! I'll go smash their car! I'm very strong, you know!
Now's not the time for joking, Benny!
Aim for the tires!
BRATATATATA
I'll report this to--
Say your prayers instead!
RATATATA TATACTAC
PIOUUUUU
WIIZZZZZ.ZZZZ
CLAC
ZZZZZZZ
CLAC
ZZZZZZZ
THE WINDSHIELD!
SMASH
Why you're crazy! Now it's freezing in this car!
Don't worry! I'm about to turn On the heat!
My turn to play!
A TIRE!
ZZZZZZZ
POW
21

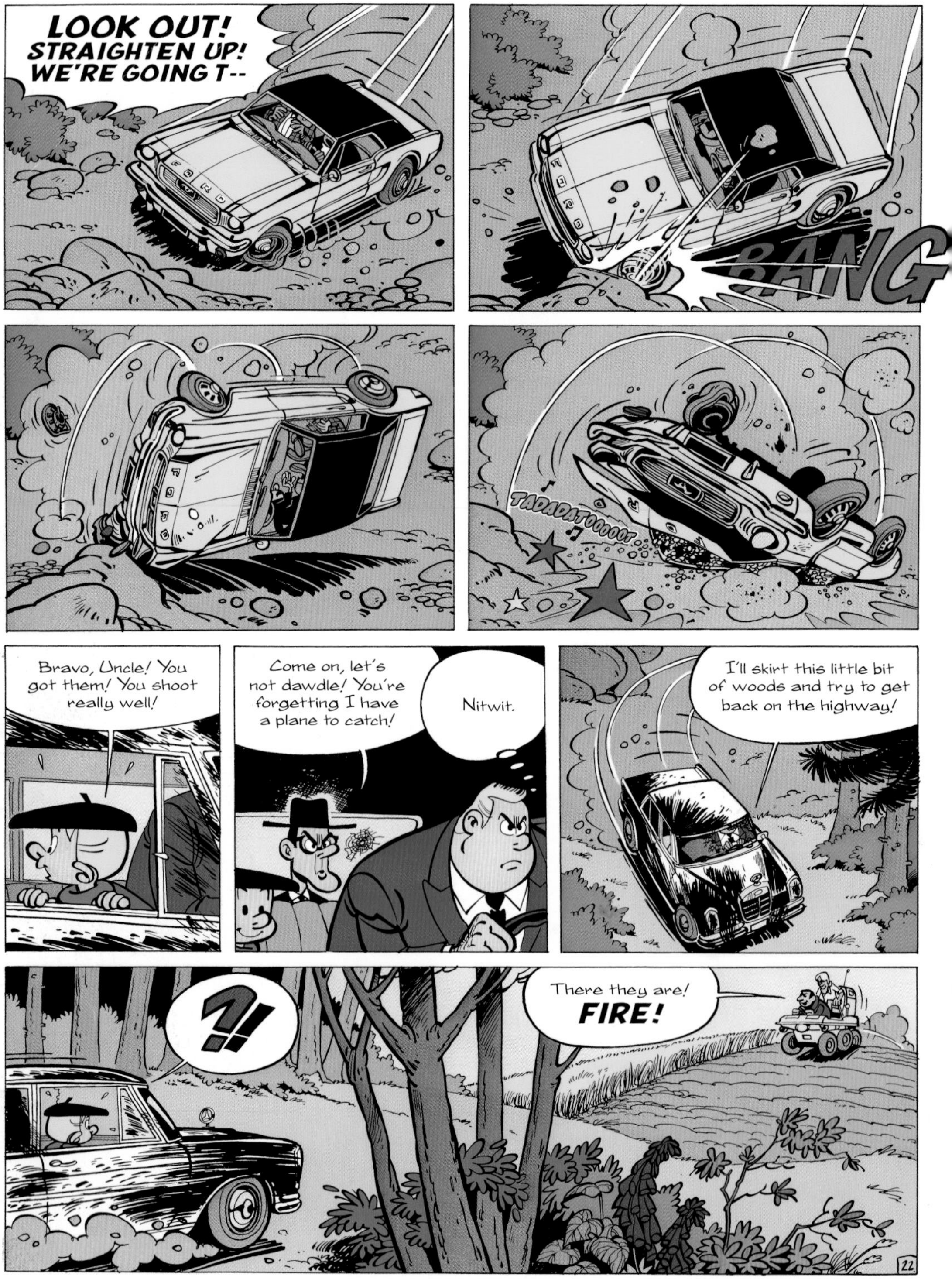
LOOK OUT! STRAIGHTEN UP! WE'RE GOING T--
FORD
BANG
TADADATOOOOOT
Bravo, Uncle! You got them! You shoot really well!
Come on, let's not dawdle! You're forgetting I have a plane to catch!
Nitwit.
I'll skirt this little bit of woods and try to get back on the highway!
?!
There they are! FIRE!
22

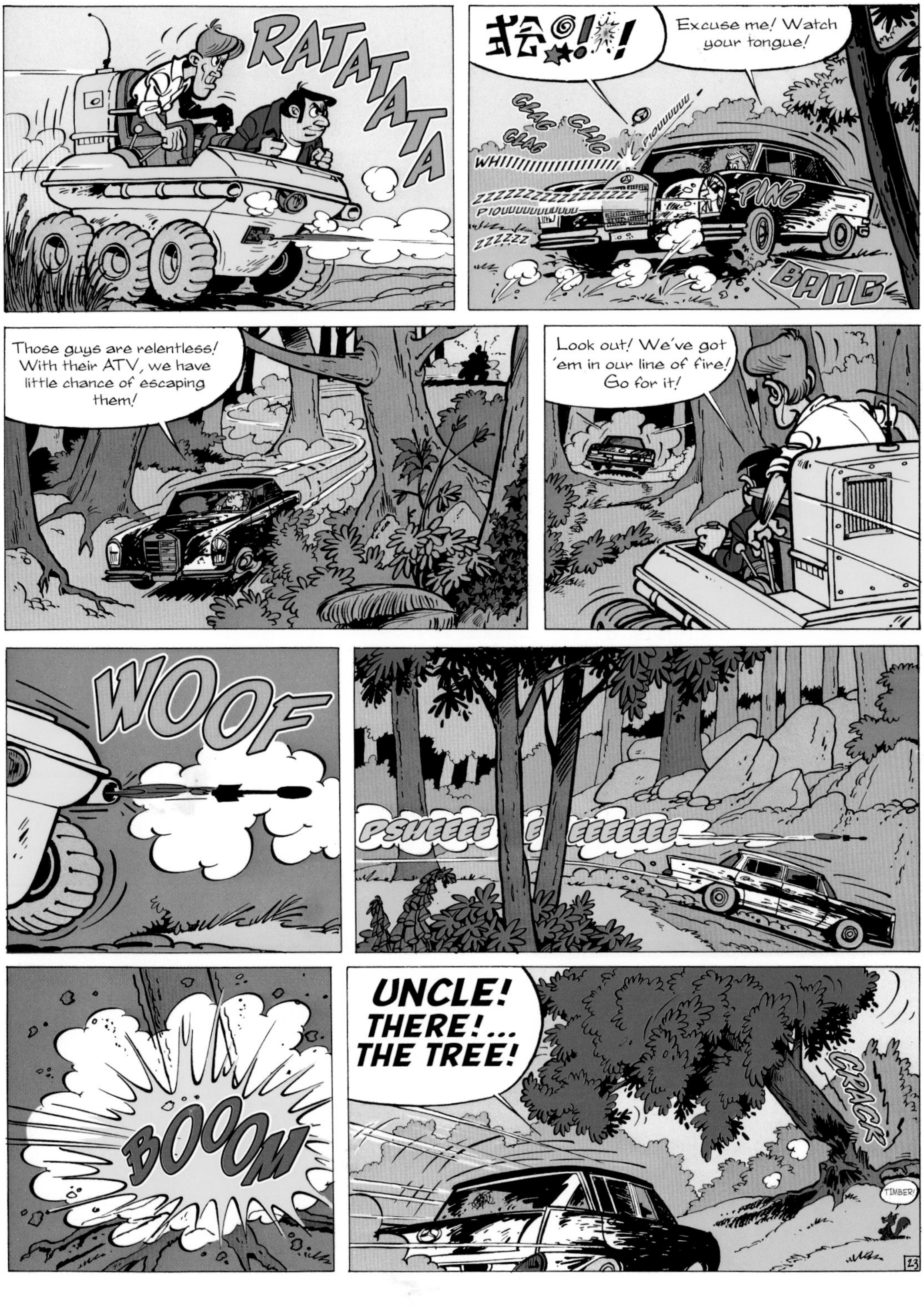

RATATATATA
Excuse me! Watch your tongue!
GLAG
CLIC
GLAG
WHIIIIIIIIIIIIIIIII
PIOUUUUUU
ZZZZZZZZZZZZZZZZZZ
PIOUUUUUUUUUUU
ZZZZZZ
PING
BANG
Those guys are relentless! With their ATV, we have little chance of escaping them!
Look out! We've got 'em in our line of fire! Go for it!
WOOF
PSHEEEEEEEEEEEEEE
BOOOM
UNCLE! THERE!... THE TREE!
CRACK
TIMBER!
23

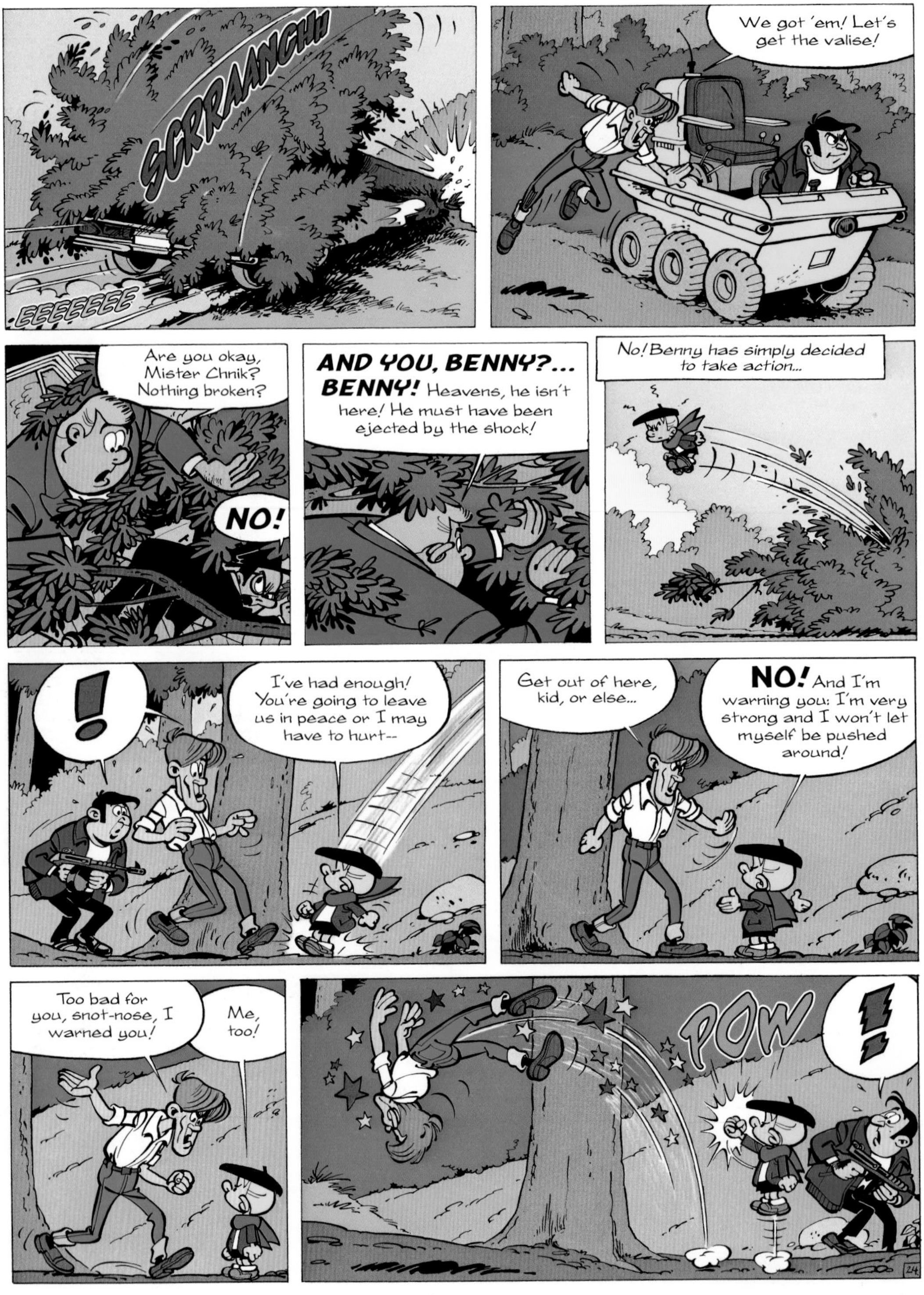
SCRRAAANCH!!
EEEEEEEE
We got 'em! Let's get the valise!
Are you okay, Mister Chnik? Nothing broken?
NO!
AND YOU, BENNY?... BENNY! Heavens, he isn't here! He must have been ejected by the shock!
No! Benny has simply decided to take action...
!
I've had enough! You're going to leave us in peace or I may have to hurt--
Get out of here, kid, or else...
NO! And I'm warning you: I'm very strong and I won't let myself be pushed around!
Too bad for you, snot-nose, I warned you!
Me, too!
POW
!

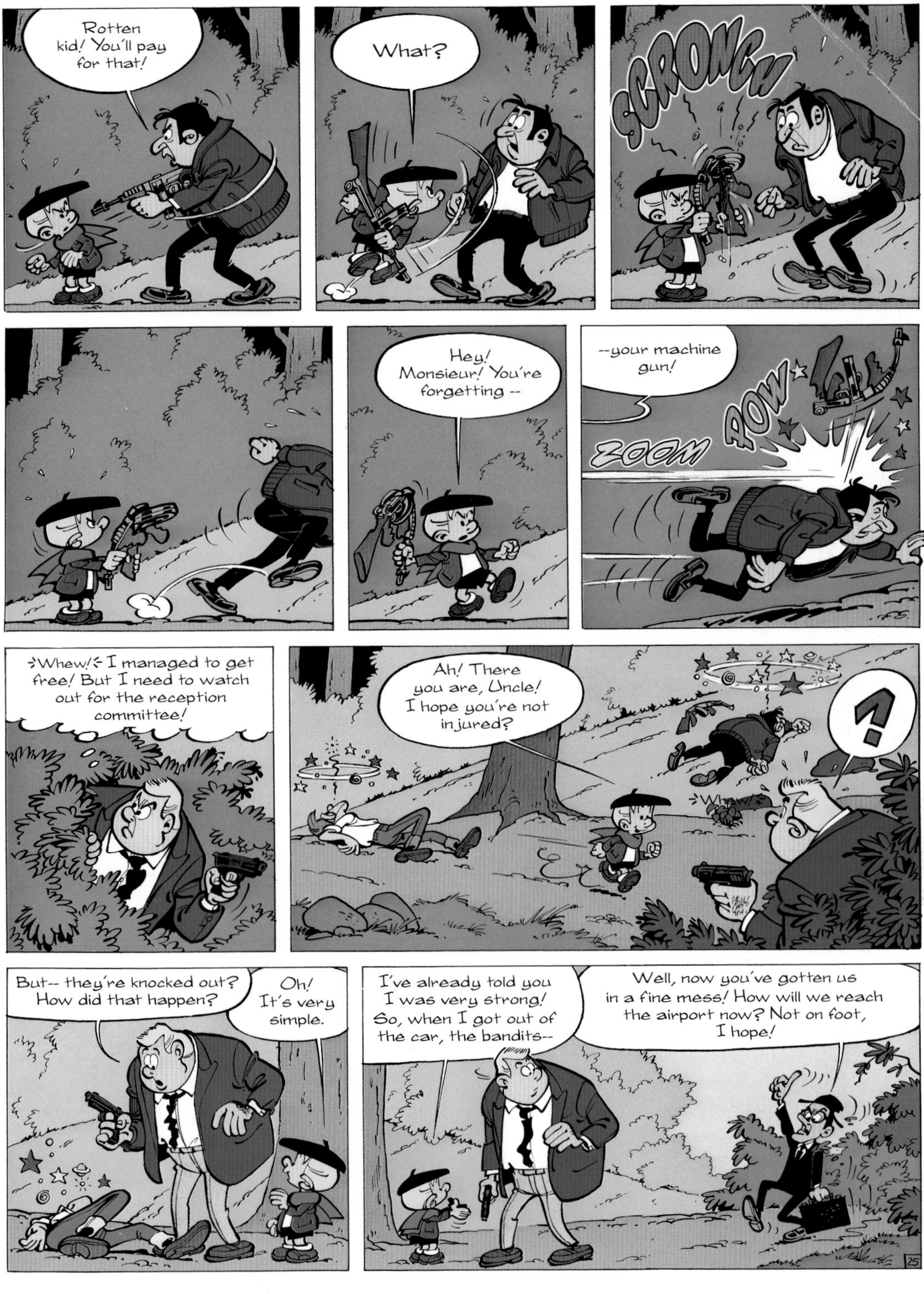
Rotten kid! You'll pay for that!
What?
SCRONCH
Hey! Monsieur! You're forgetting --
--your machine gun!
POW
ZOOM
Whew! I managed to get free! But I need to watch out for the reception committee!
Ah! There you are, Uncle! I hope you're not injured?
?
Whew!
But-- they're knocked out? How did that happen?
Oh! It's very simple.
I've already told you I was very strong! So, when I got out of the car, the bandits--
Well, now you've gotten us in a fine mess! How will we reach the airport now? Not on foot, I hope!
25

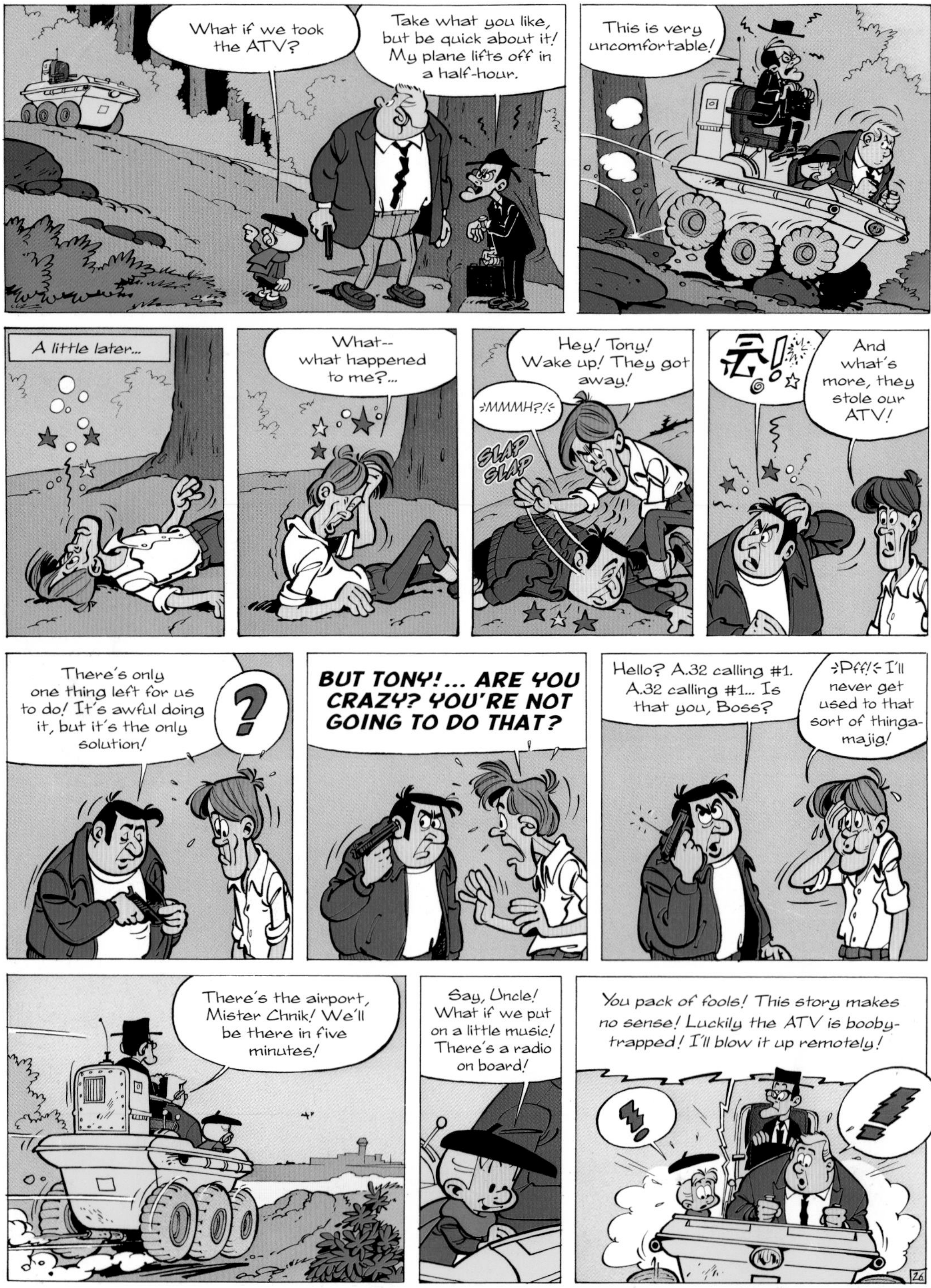

What if we took the ATV?
Take what you like, but be quick about it! My plane lifts off in a half-hour.
This is very uncomfortable!
A little later...
What-- what happened to me?...
Hey! Tony! Wake up! They got away!
MMMH?!
SLAP SLAP
And what's more, they stole our ATV!
There's only one thing left for us to do! It's awful doing it, but it's the only solution!
?
BUT TONY!... ARE YOU CRAZY? YOU'RE NOT GOING TO DO THAT?
Hello? A.32 calling #1. A.32 calling #1... Is that you, Boss?
Pff! I'll never get used to that sort of thinga-majig!
There's the airport, Mister Chnik! We'll be there in five minutes!
Say, Uncle! What if we put on a little music! There's a radio on board!
You pack of fools! This story makes no sense! Luckily the ATV is booby-trapped! I'll blow it up remotely!
26

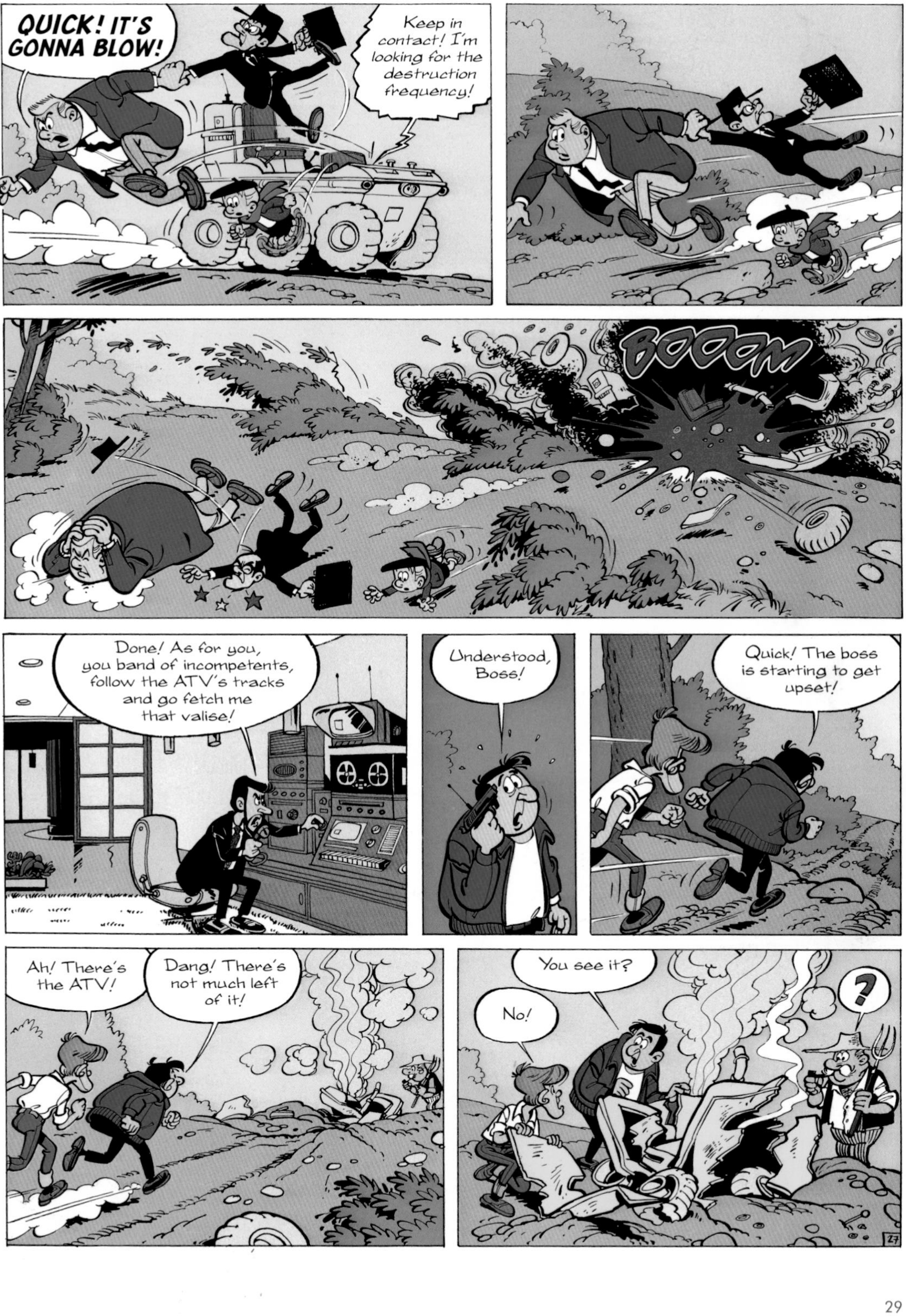
QUICK! IT'S GONNA BLOW!
Keep in contact! I'm looking for the destruction frequency!
BOOOM
Done! As for you, you band of incompetents, follow the ATV's tracks and go fetch me that valise!
Understood, Boss!
Quick! The boss is starting to get upset!
Ah! There's the ATV!
Dang! There's not much left of it!
You see it?
No!
?
27

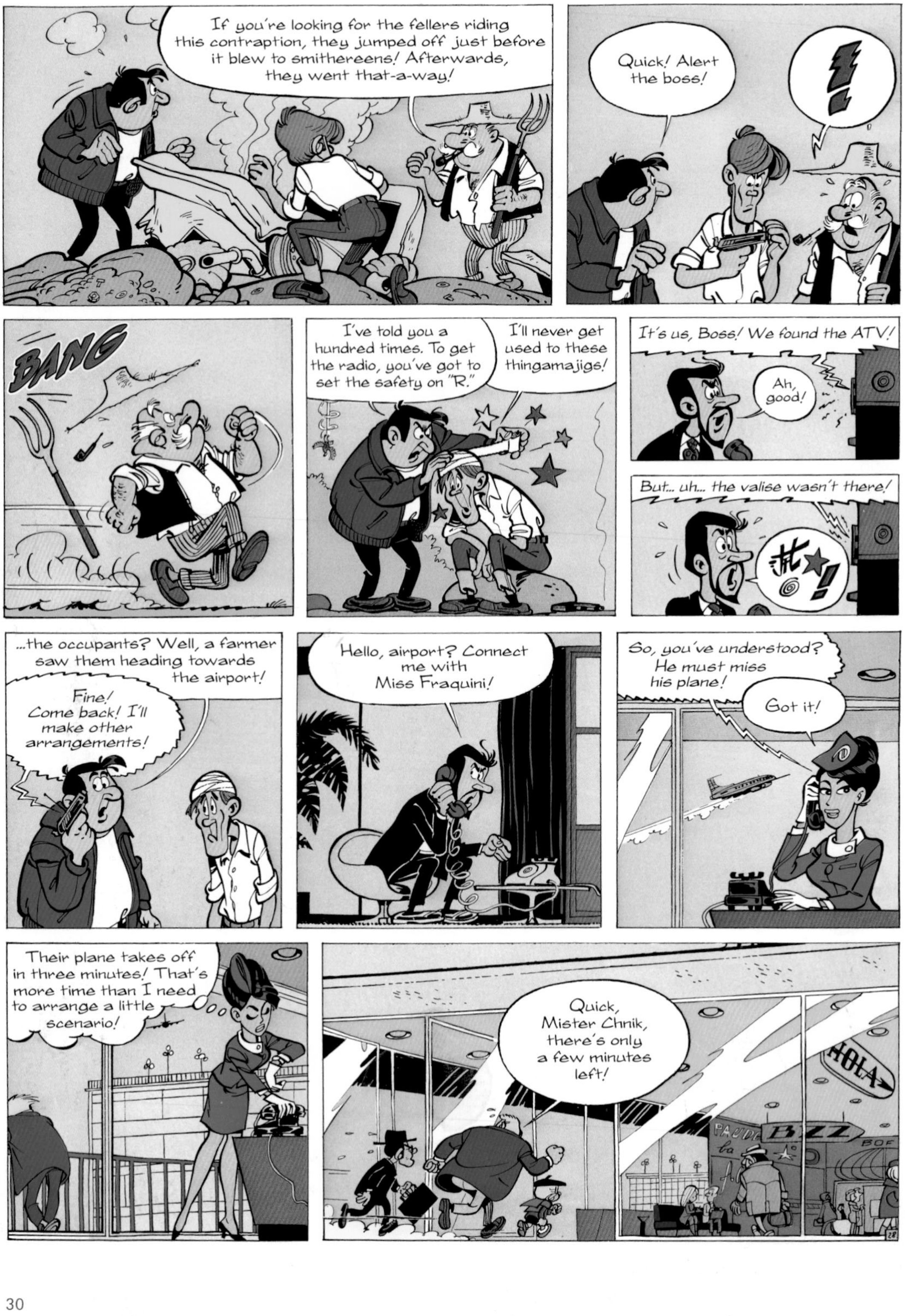
If you're looking for the fellers riding this contraption, they jumped off just before it blew to smithereens! Afterwards, they went that-a-way!
Quick! Alert the boss!
BANG
I've told you a hundred times. To get the radio, you've got to set the safety on "R."
I'll never get used to these thingamajigs!
It's us, Boss! We found the ATV!
Ah, good!
But... uh... the valise wasn't there!
...the occupants? Well, a farmer saw them heading towards the airport!
Fine! Come back! I'll make other arrangements!
Hello, airport? Connect me with Miss Fraquini!
So, you've understood? He must miss his plane!
Got it!
Their plane takes off in three minutes! That's more time than I need to arrange a little scenario!
Quick, Mister Chnik, there's only a few minutes left!
HOLA
BZZ
BOF

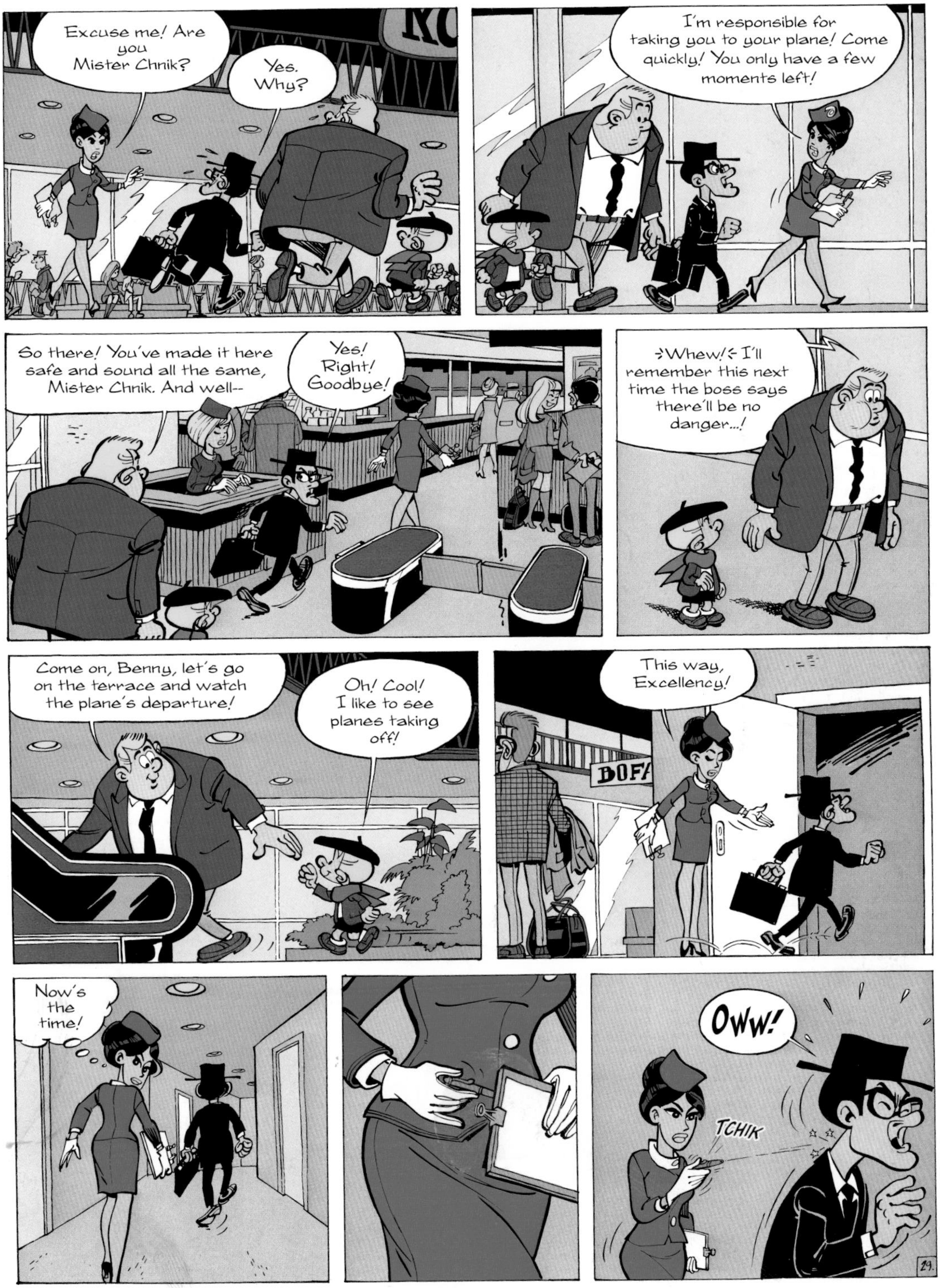

Excuse me! Are you Mister Chnik?
Yes. Why?
I'm responsible for taking you to your plane! Come quickly! You only have a few moments left!
So there! You've made it here safe and sound all the same, Mister Chnik. And well--
Yes! Right! Goodbye!
Whew! I'll remember this next time the boss says there'll be no danger...!
Come on, Benny, let's go on the terrace and watch the plane's departure!
Oh! Cool! I like to see planes taking off!
This way, Excellency!
BOF
Now's the time!
OWW!
TCHIK

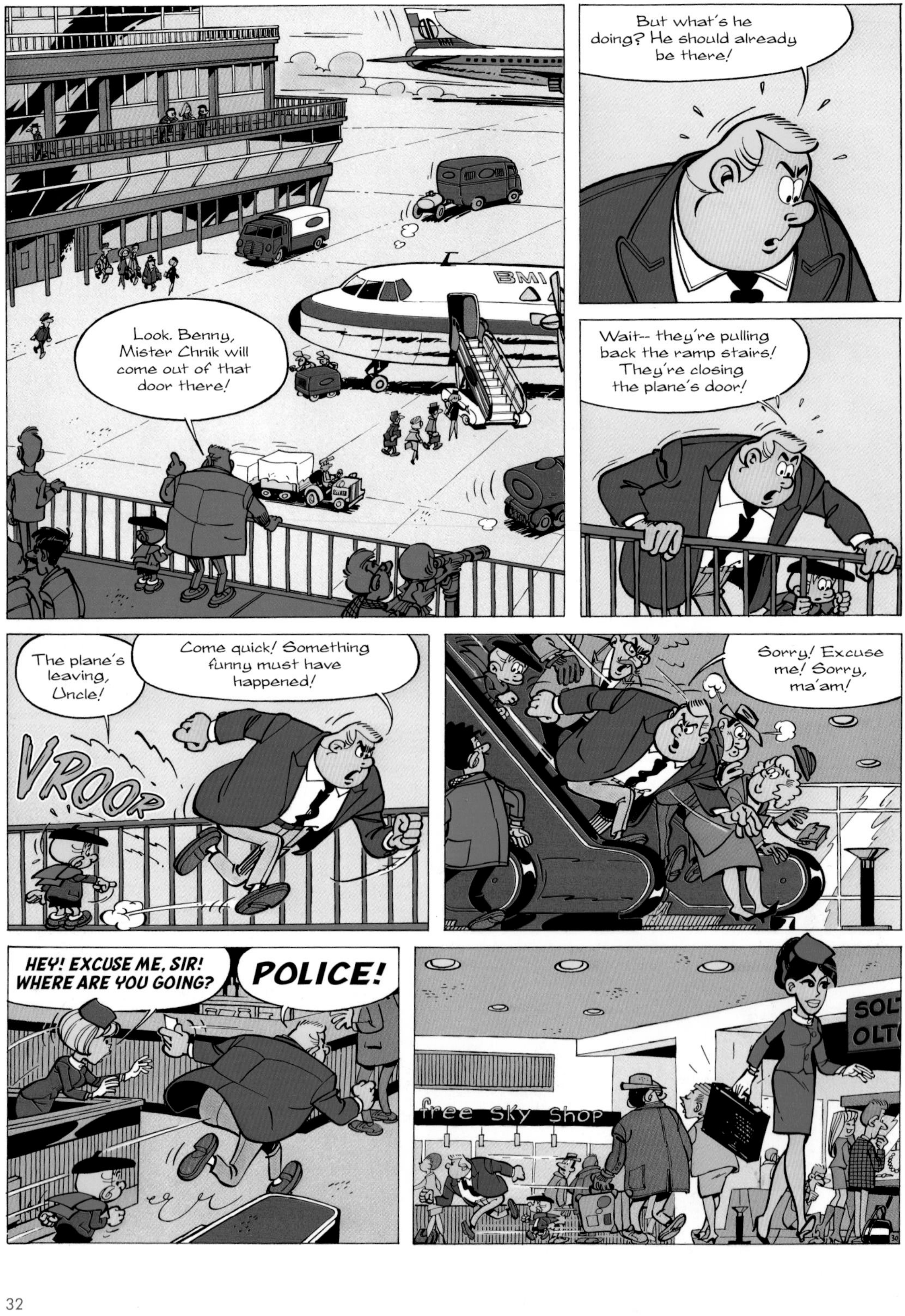

BMI
Look. Benny, Mister Chnik will come out of that door there!
But what's he doing? He should already be there!
Wait-- they're pulling back the ramp stairs! They're closing the plane's door!
The plane's leaving, Uncle!
Come quick! Something funny must have happened!
VROOR
Sorry! Excuse me! Sorry, ma'am!
HEY! EXCUSE ME, SIR! WHERE ARE YOU GOING?
POLICE!
free sky shop

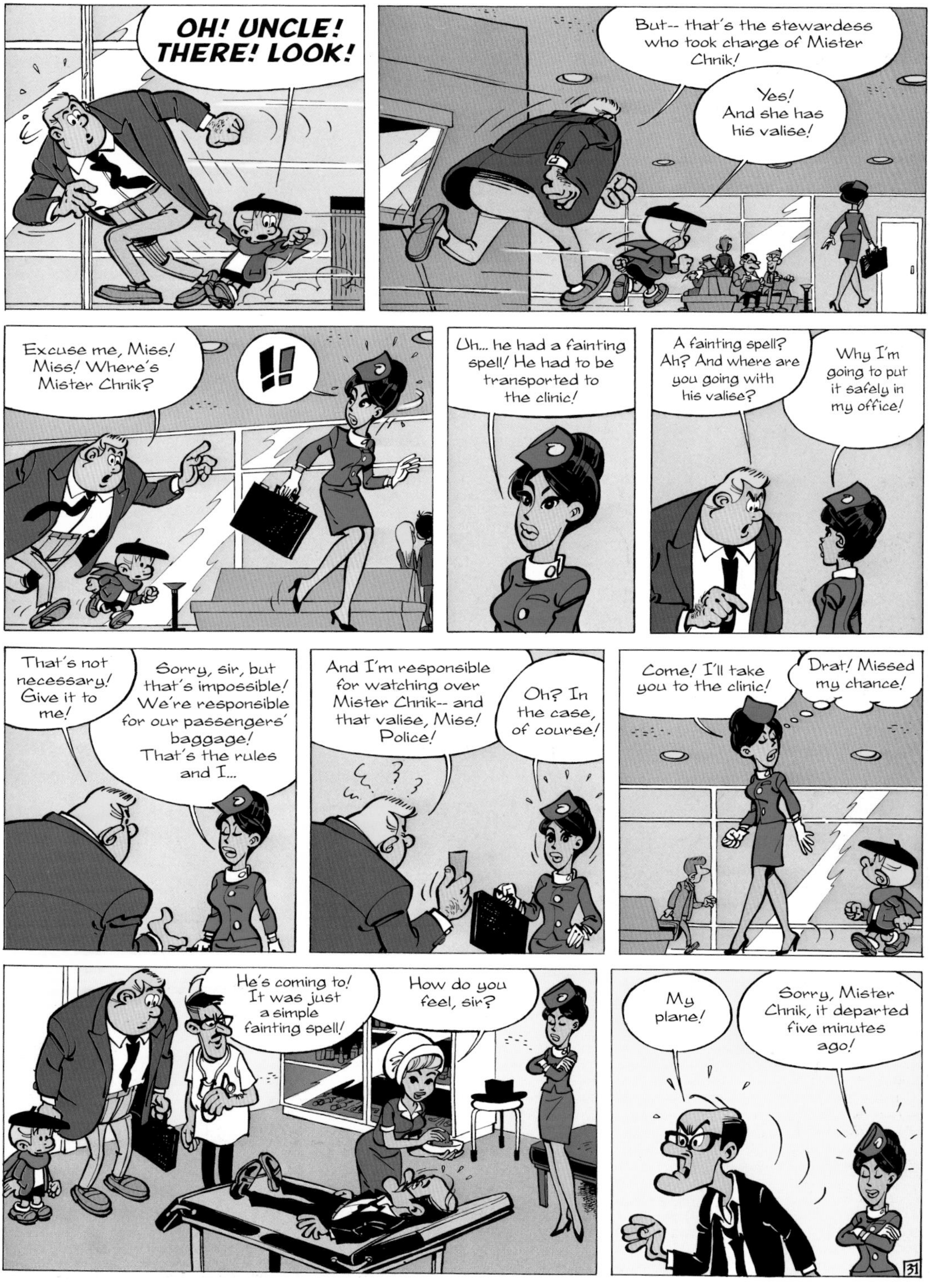
OH! UNCLE! THERE! LOOK!
But-- that's the stewardess who took charge of Mister Chnik!
Yes! And she has his valise!
Excuse me, Miss! Miss! Where's Mister Chnik?
!!
Uh... he had a fainting spell! He had to be transported to the clinic!
A fainting spell? Ah? And where are you going with his valise?
Why I'm going to put it safely in my office!
That's not necessary! Give it to me!
Sorry, sir, but that's impossible! We're responsible for our passengers' baggage! That's the rules and I...
And I'm responsible for watching over Mister Chnik-- and that valise, Miss! Police!
Oh? In the case, of course!
Come! I'll take you to the clinic!
Drat! Missed my chance!
He's coming to! It was just a simple fainting spell!
How do you feel, sir?
My plane!
Sorry, Mister Chnik, it departed five minutes ago!
31

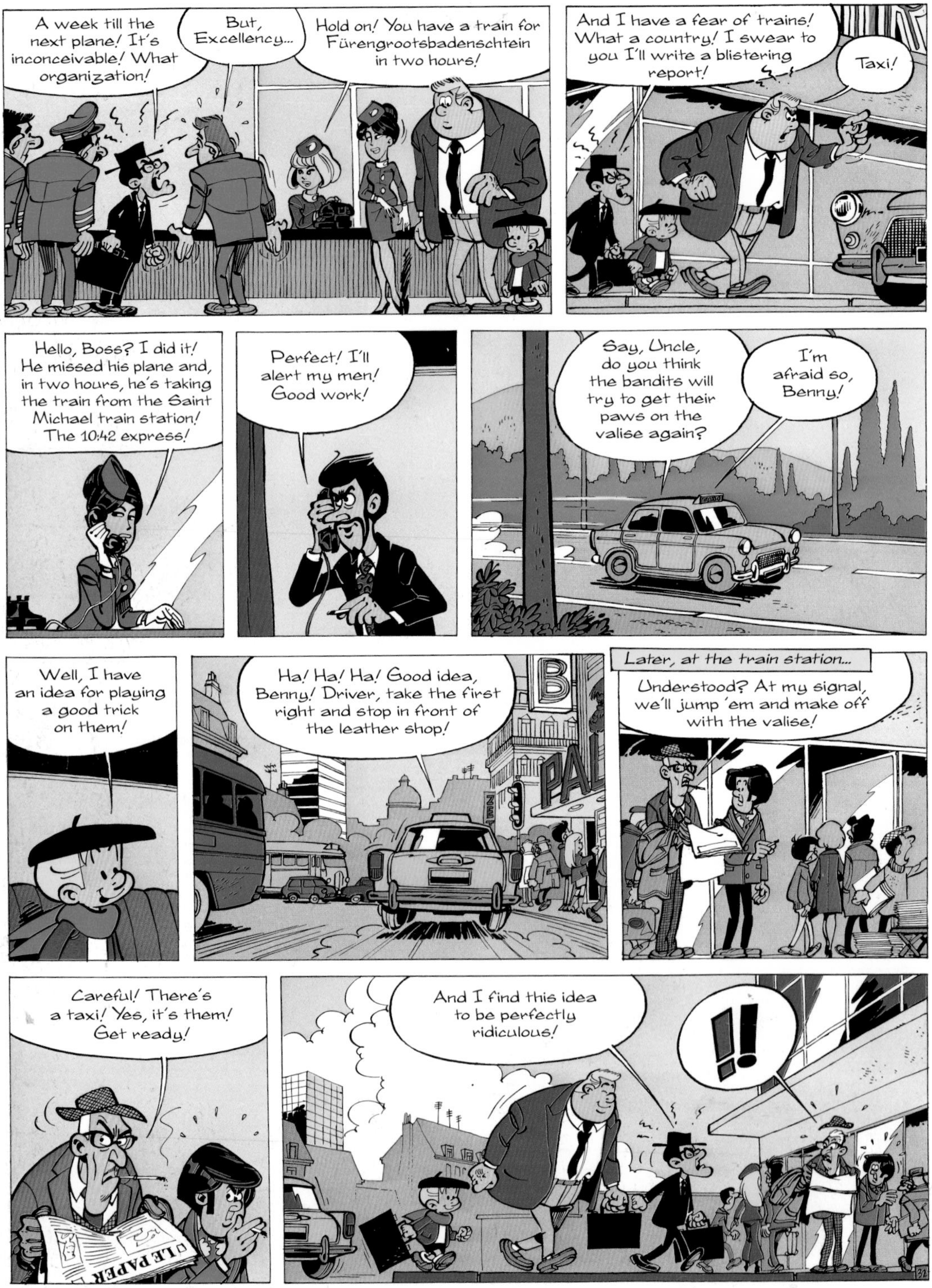
A week till the next plane! It's inconceivable! What organization!
But, Excellency...
Hold on! You have a train for Fürengrootsbadenschtein in two hours!
And I have a fear of trains! What a country! I swear to you I'll write a blistering report!
Taxi!
Hello, Boss? I did it! He missed his plane and, in two hours, he's taking the train from the Saint Michael train station! The 10:42 express!
Perfect! I'll alert my men! Good work!
Say, Uncle, do you think the bandits will try to get their paws on the valise again?
I'm afraid so, Benny!
Well, I have an idea for playing a good trick on them!
Ha! Ha! Ha! Good idea, Benny! Driver, take the first right and stop in front of the leather shop!
Later, at the train station...
Understood? At my signal, we'll jump 'em and make off with the valise!
Careful! There's a taxi! Yes, it's them! Get ready!
LE PAPER
And I find this idea to be perfectly ridiculous!
!!

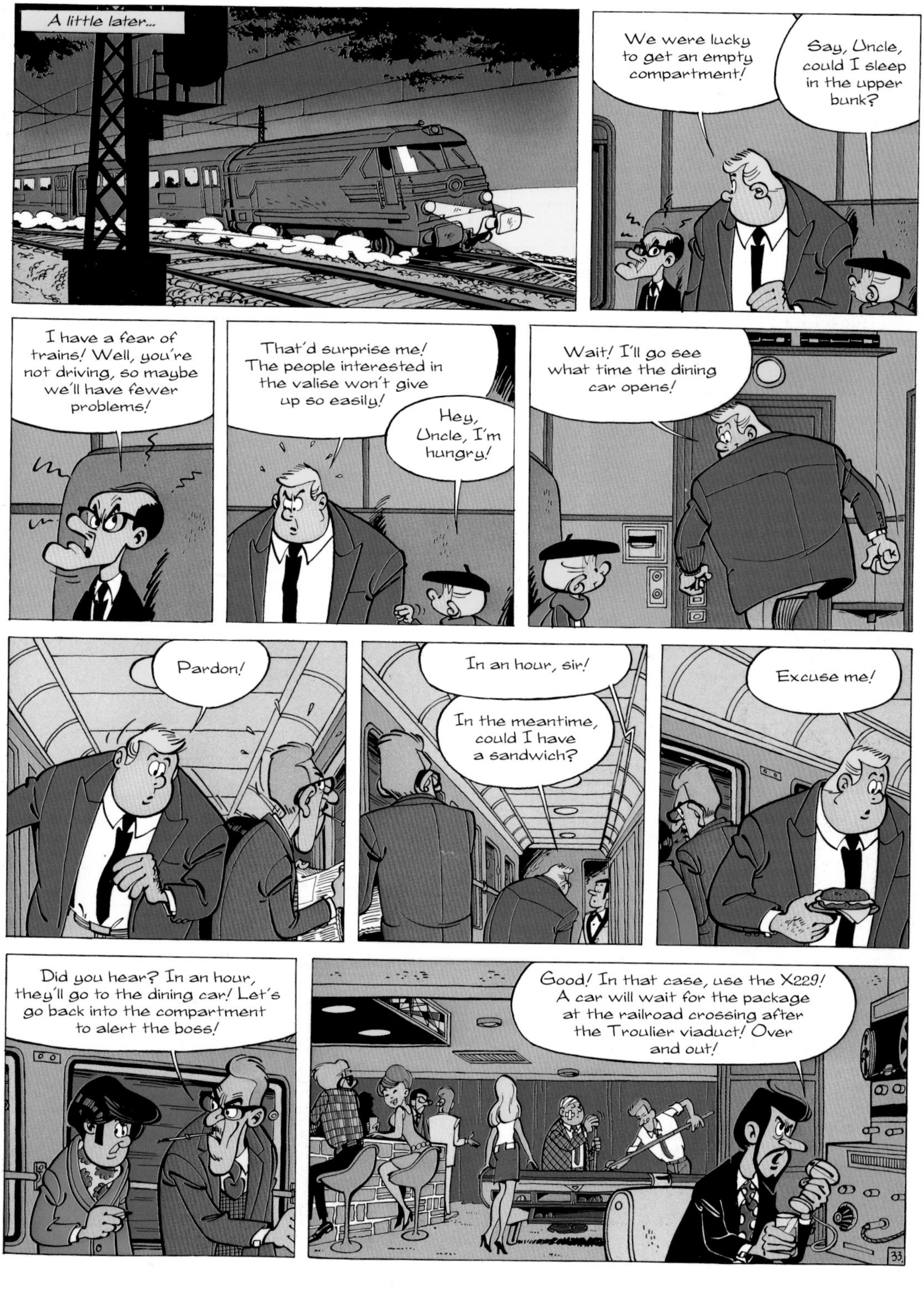
A little later...
We were lucky to get an empty compartment!
Say, Uncle, could I sleep in the upper bunk?
I have a fear of trains! Well, you're not driving, so maybe we'll have fewer problems!
That'd surprise me! The people interested in the valise won't give up so easily!
Hey, Uncle, I'm hungry!
Wait! I'll go see what time the dining car opens!
Pardon!
In an hour, sir!
In the meantime, could I have a sandwich?
Excuse me!
Did you hear? In an hour, they'll go to the dining car! Let's go back into the compartment to alert the boss!
Good! In that case, use the X229! A car will wait for the package at the railroad crossing after the Troulier viaduct! Over and out!
33

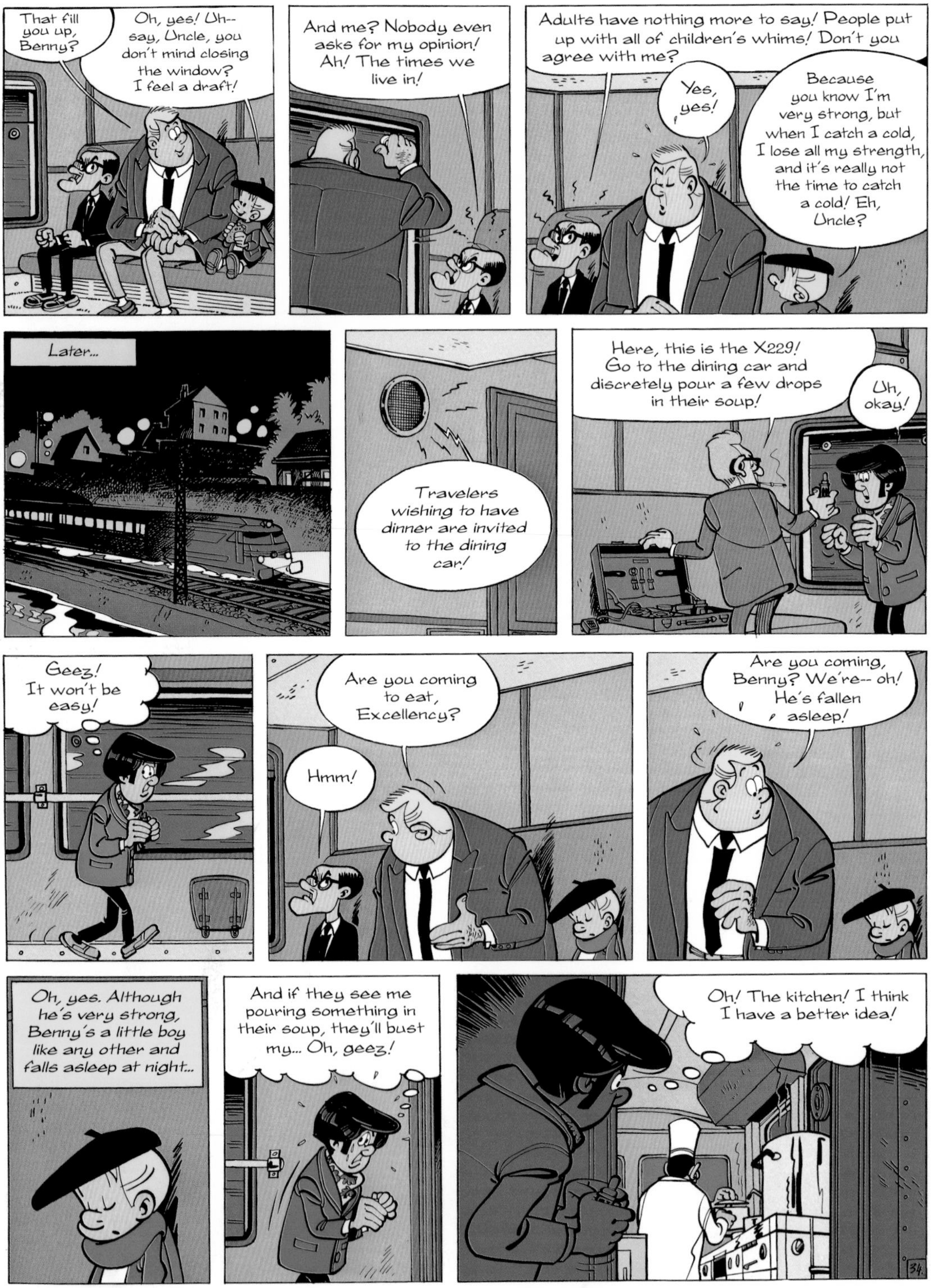
That fill you up, Benny?
Oh, yes! Uh-- say, Uncle, you don't mind closing the window? I feel a draft!
And me? Nobody even asks for my opinion! Ah! The times we live in!
Adults have nothing more to say! People put up with all of children's whims! Don't you agree with me?
Yes, yes!
Because you know I'm very strong, but when I catch a cold, I lose all my strength, and it's really not the time to catch a cold! Eh, Uncle?
Later...
Travelers wishing to have dinner are invited to the dining car!
Here, this is the X229! Go to the dining car and discretely pour a few drops in their soup!
Uh, okay!
Geez! It won't be easy!
Are you coming to eat, Excellency?
Hmm!
Are you coming, Benny? We're-- oh! He's fallen asleep!
Oh, yes. Although he's very strong, Benny's a little boy like any other and falls asleep at night...
And if they see me pouring something in their soup, they'll bust my... Oh, geez!
Oh! The kitchen! I think I have a better idea!
34.

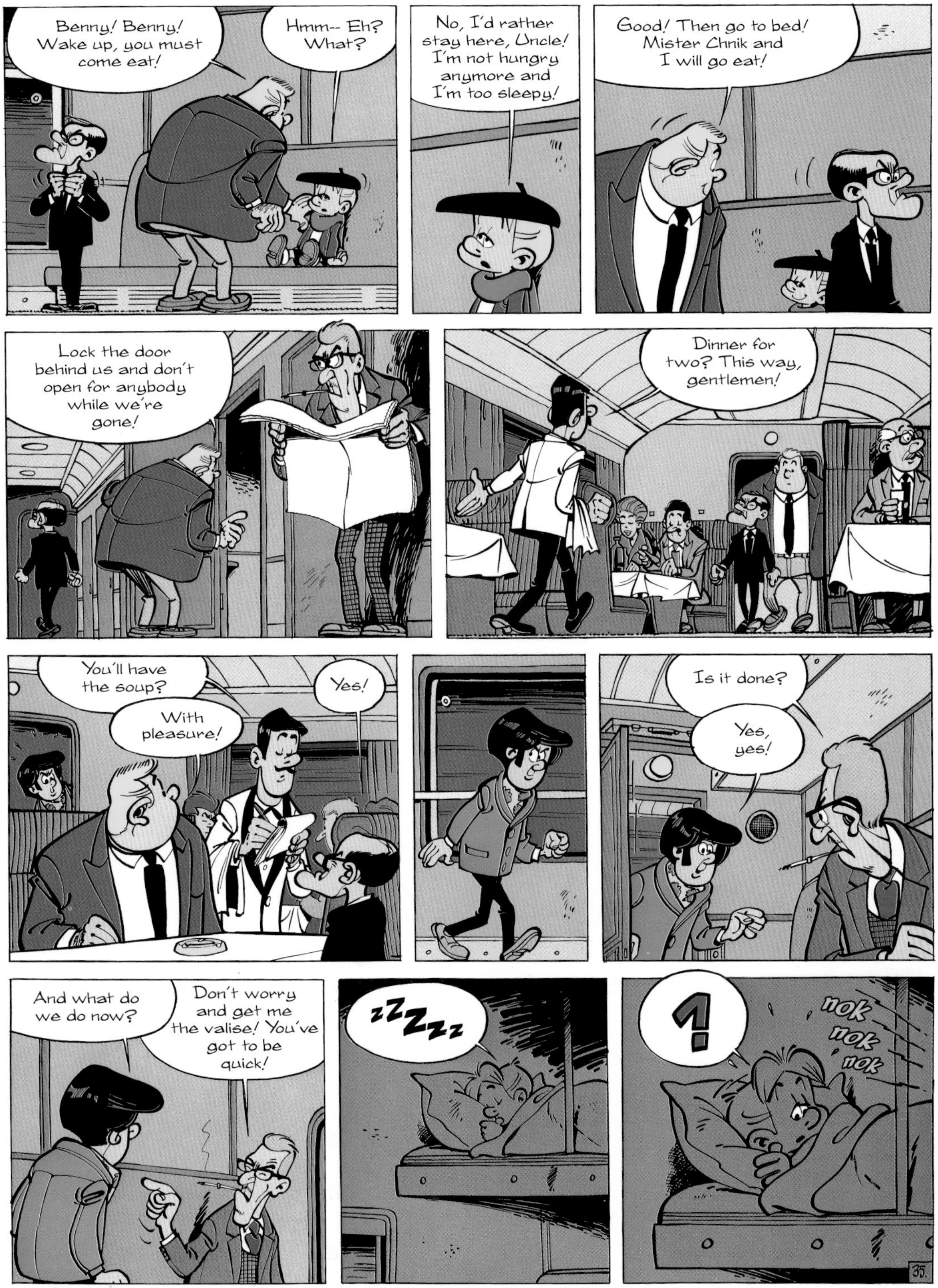

Benny! Benny! Wake up, you must come eat!
Hmm-- Eh? What?
No, I'd rather stay here, Uncle! I'm not hungry anymore and I'm too sleepy!
Good! Then go to bed! Mister Chnik and I will go eat!
Lock the door behind us and don't open for anybody while we're gone!
Dinner for two? This way, gentlemen!
You'll have the soup?
With pleasure!
Yes!
Is it done?
Yes, yes!
And what do we do now?
Don't worry and get me the valise! You've got to be quick!
zzZzzz
?
nok nok nok
35.

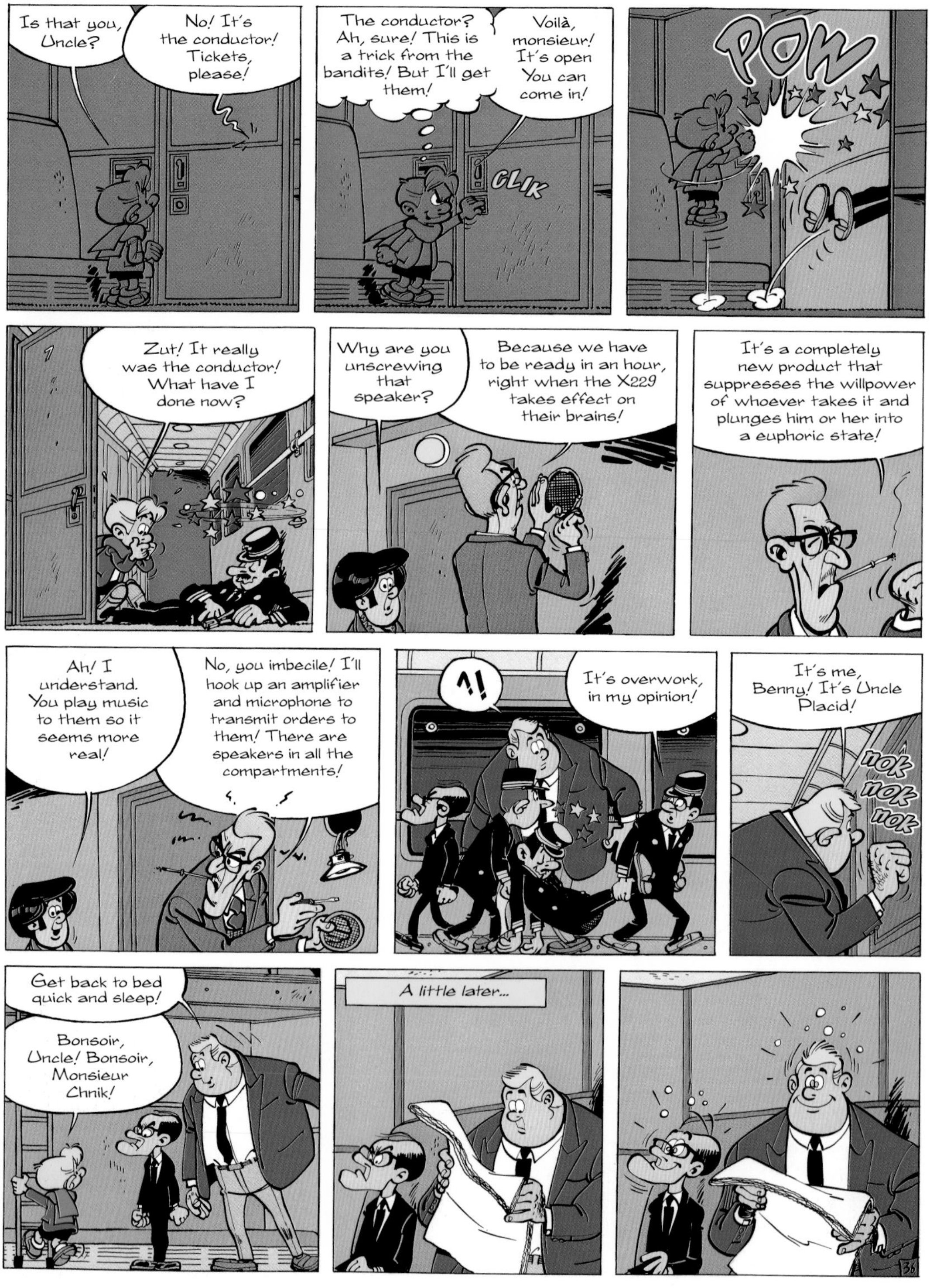
Is that you, Uncle?
No! It's the conductor! Tickets, please!
The conductor? Ah, sure! This is a trick from the bandits! But I'll get them!
Voilà, monsieur! It's open You can come in!
CLIK
POW
Zut! It really was the conductor! What have I done now?
Why are you unscrewing that speaker?
Because we have to be ready in an hour, right when the X229 takes effect on their brains!
It's a completely new product that suppresses the willpower of whoever takes it and plunges him or her into a euphoric state!
Ah! I understand. You play music to them so it seems more real!
No, you imbecile! I'll hook up an amplifier and microphone to transmit orders to them! There are speakers in all the compartments!
?!
It's overwork, in my opinion!
It's me, Benny! It's Uncle Placid!
nok nok nok
Get back to bed quick and sleep!
Bonsoir, Uncle! Bonsoir, Monsieur Chnik!
A little later...

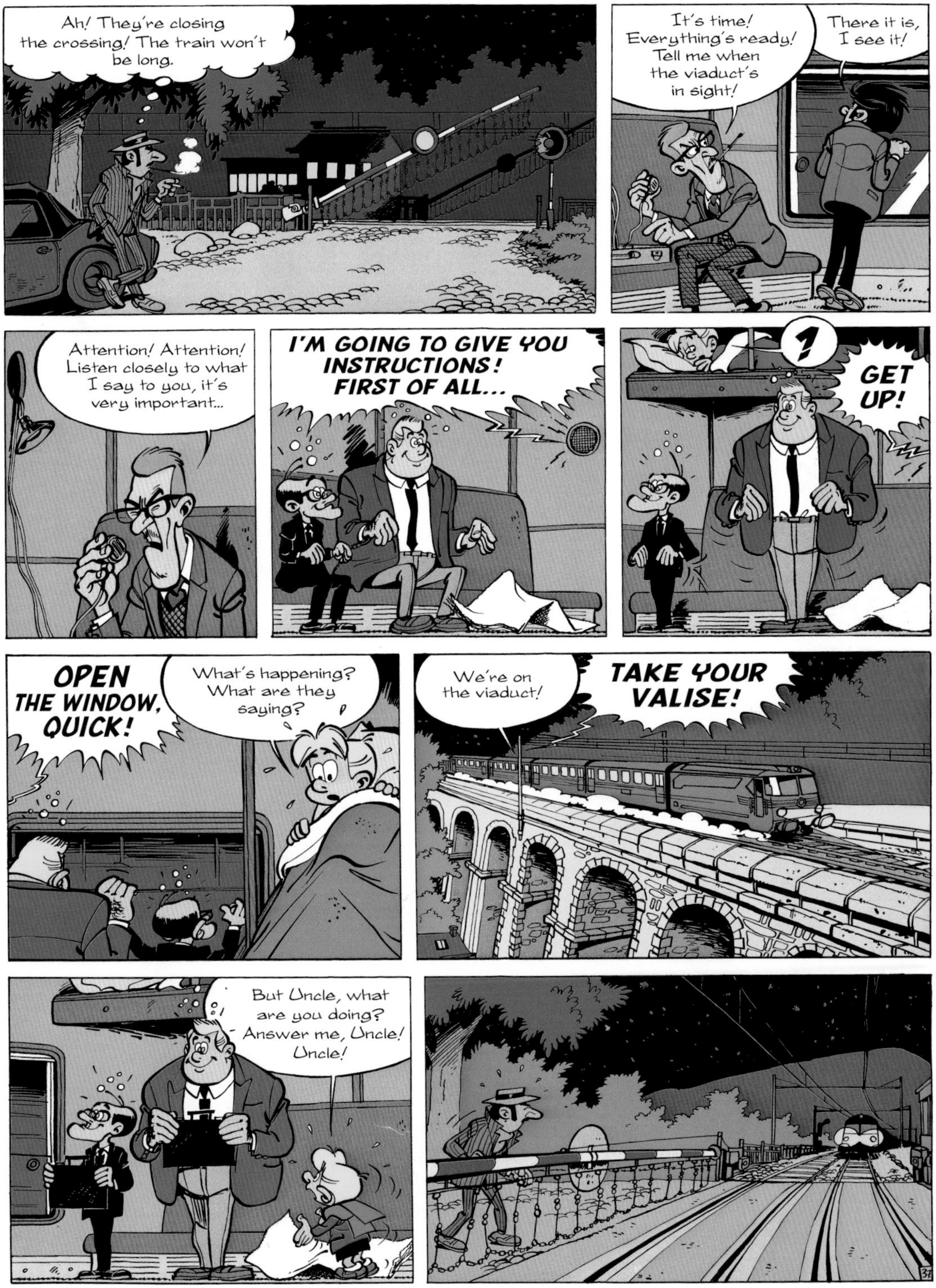

Ah! They're closing the crossing! The train won't be long.
It's time! Everything's ready! Tell me when the viaduct's in sight!
There it is, I see it!
Attention! Attention! Listen closely to what I say to you, it's very important...
I'M GOING TO GIVE YOU INSTRUCTIONS! FIRST OF ALL...
?
GET UP!
OPEN THE WINDOW, QUICK!
What's happening? What are they saying?
We're on the viaduct!
TAKE YOUR VALISE!
But Uncle, what are you doing? Answer me, Uncle! Uncle!
37

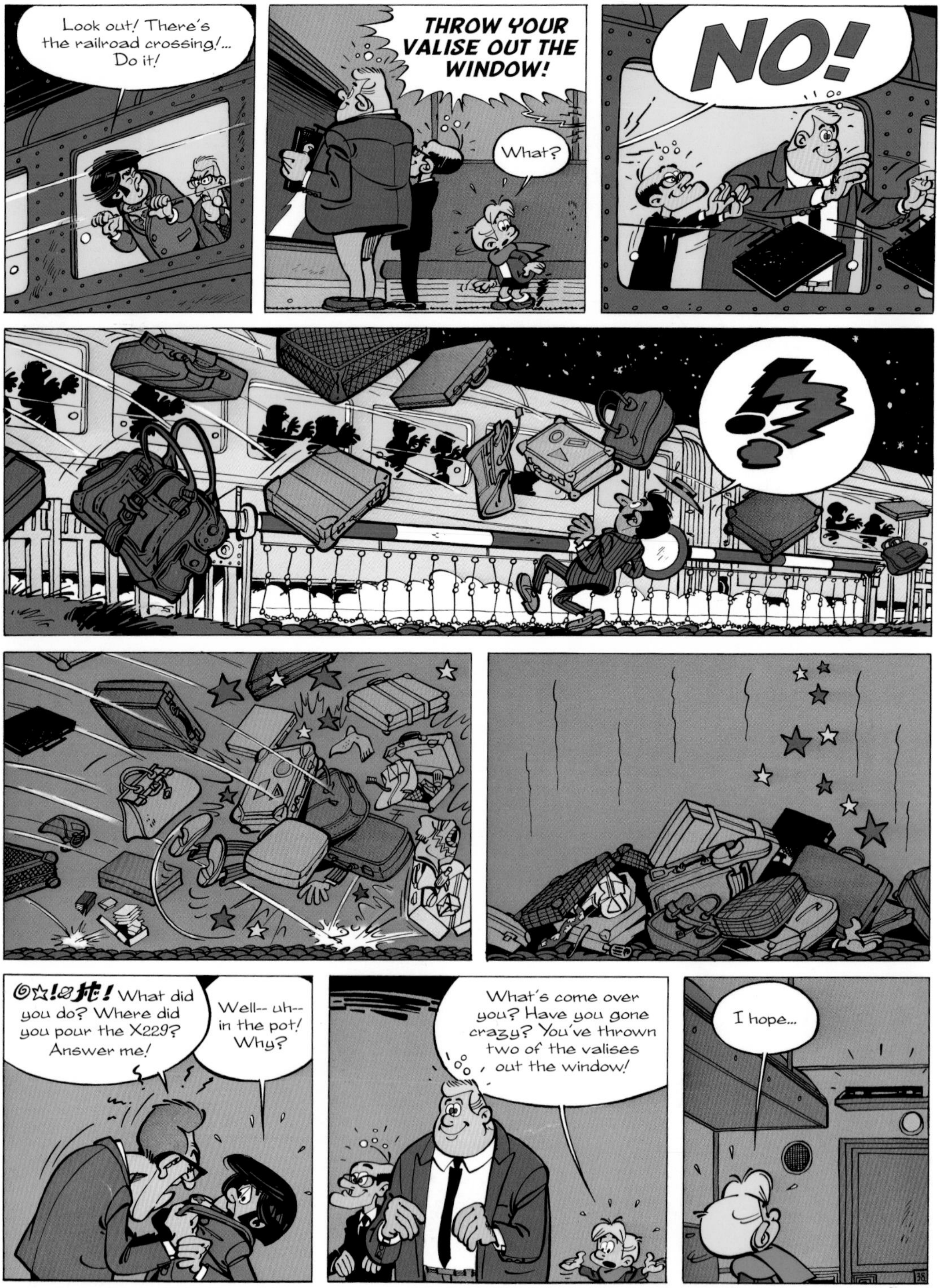
Look out! There's the railroad crossing!... Do it!
THROW YOUR VALISE OUT THE WINDOW!
What?
NO!
What did you do? Where did you pour the X229? Answer me!
Well-- uh-- in the pot! Why?
What's come over you? Have you gone crazy? You've thrown two of the valises out the window!
I hope...
38

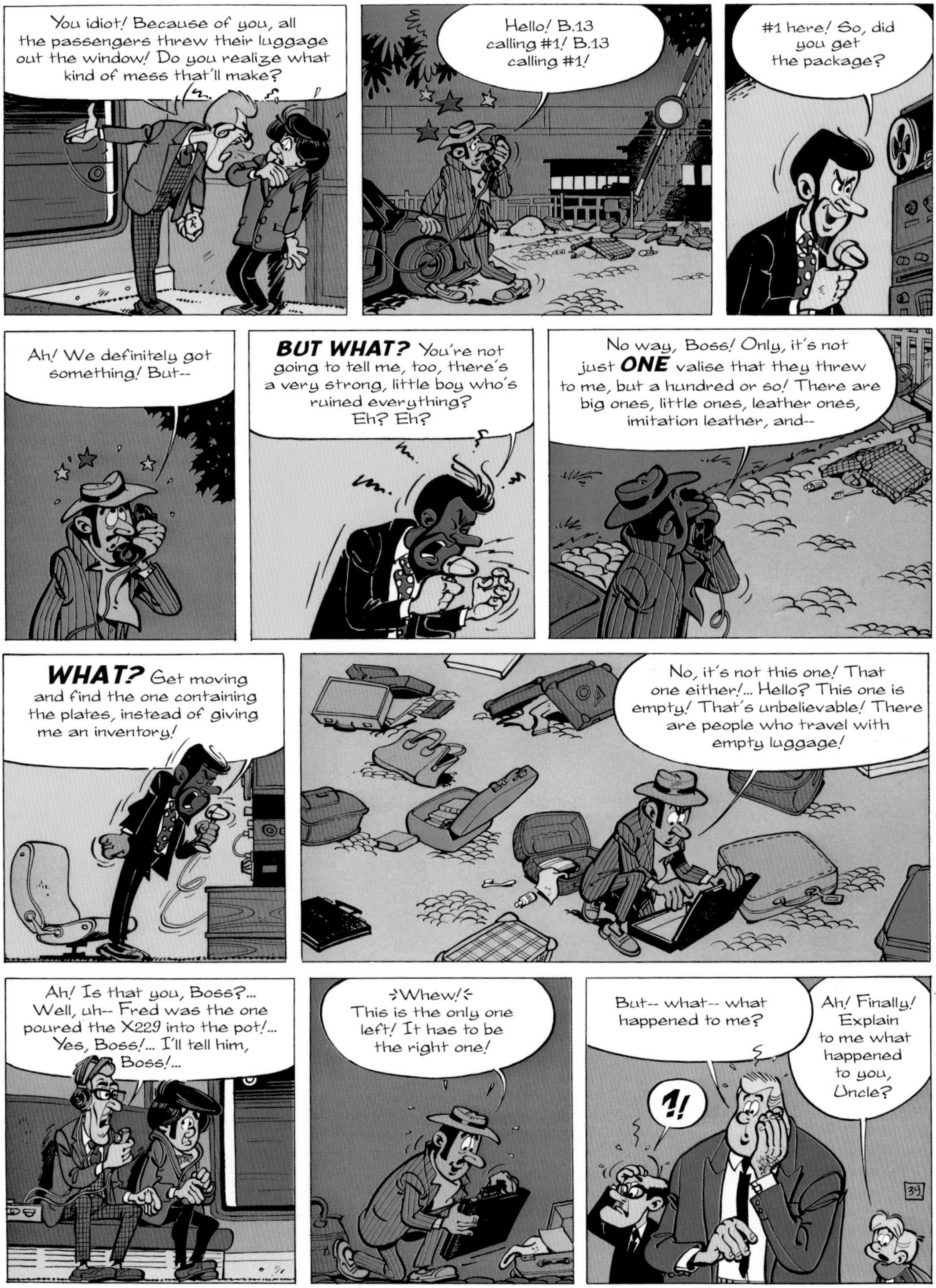
You idiot! Because of you, all the passengers threw their luggage out the window! Do you realize what kind of mess that'll make?
Hello! B.13 calling #1! B.13 calling #1!
#1 here! So, did you get the package?
Ah! We definitely got something! But--
BUT WHAT? You're not going to tell me, too, there's a very strong, little boy who's ruined everything? Eh? Eh?
No way, Boss! Only, it's not just ONE valise that they threw to me, but a hundred or so! There are big ones, little ones, leather ones, imitation leather, and--
WHAT? Get moving and find the one containing the plates, instead of giving me an inventory!
No, it's not this one! That one either!... Hello? This one is empty! That's unbelievable! There are people who travel with empty luggage!
Ah! Is that you, Boss?... Well, uh-- Fred was the one poured the X229 into the pot!... Yes, Boss!... I'll tell him, Boss!...
Whew! This is the only one left! It has to be the right one!
But-- what-- what happened to me?
Ah! Finally! Explain to me what happened to you, Uncle?
!!
39

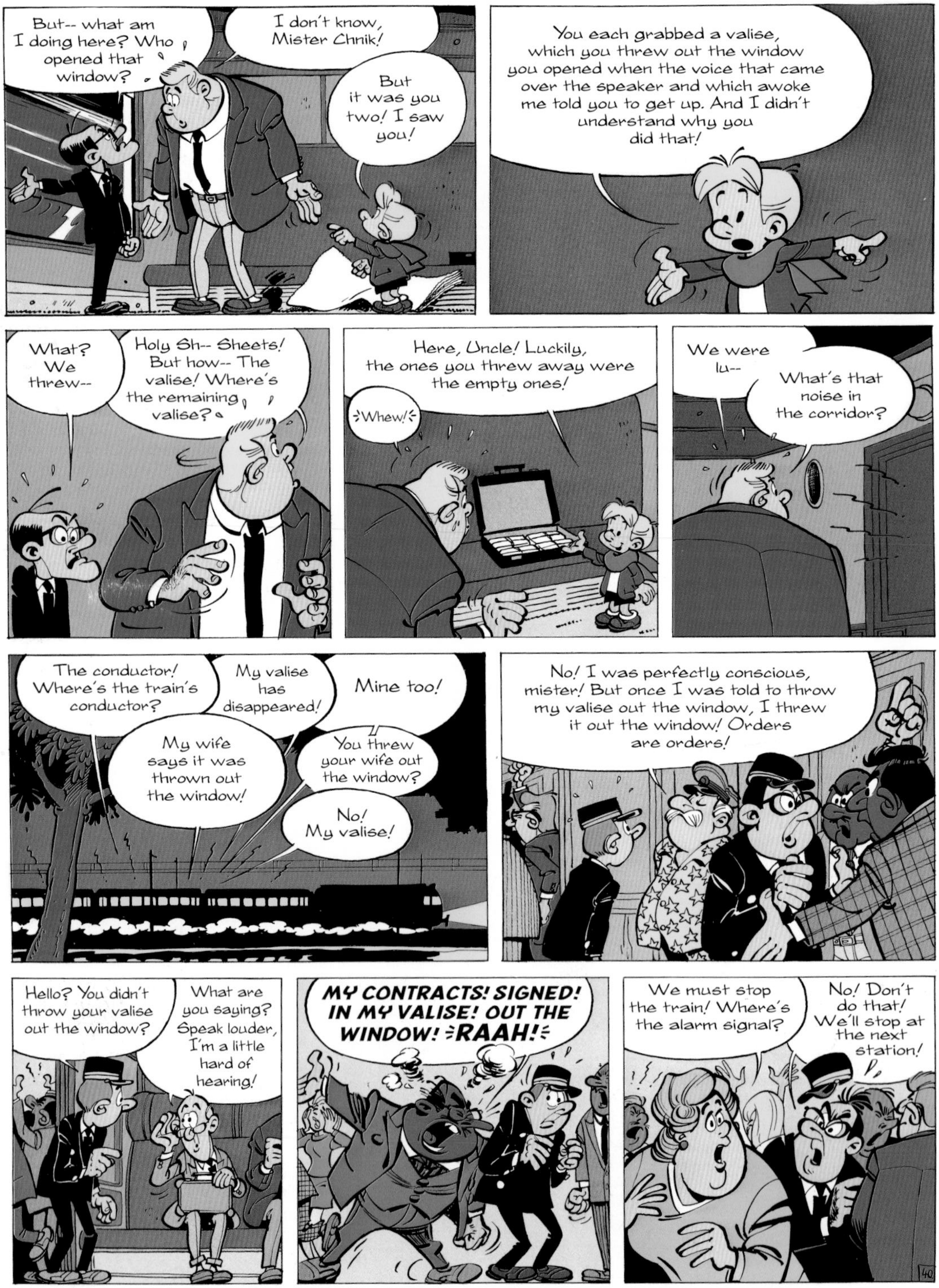
But-- what am I doing here? Who opened that window?
I don't know, Mister Chnik!
But it was you two! I saw you!
You each grabbed a valise, which you threw out the window you opened when the voice that came over the speaker and which awoke me told you to get up. And I didn't understand why you did that!
What? We threw--
Holy Sh-- Sheets! But how-- The valise! Where's the remaining valise?
Here, Uncle! Luckily, the ones you threw away were the empty ones!
Whew!
We were lu--
What's that noise in the corridor?
The conductor! Where's the train's conductor?
My valise has disappeared!
Mine too!
My wife says it was thrown out the window!
You threw your wife out the window?
No! My valise!
No! I was perfectly conscious, mister! But once I was told to throw my valise out the window, I threw it out the window! Orders are orders!
Hello? You didn't throw your valise out the window?
What are you saying? Speak louder, I'm a little hard of hearing!
MY CONTRACTS! SIGNED! IN MY VALISE! OUT THE WINDOW! RAAH!
We must stop the train! Where's the alarm signal?
No! Don't do that! We'll stop at the next station!
40

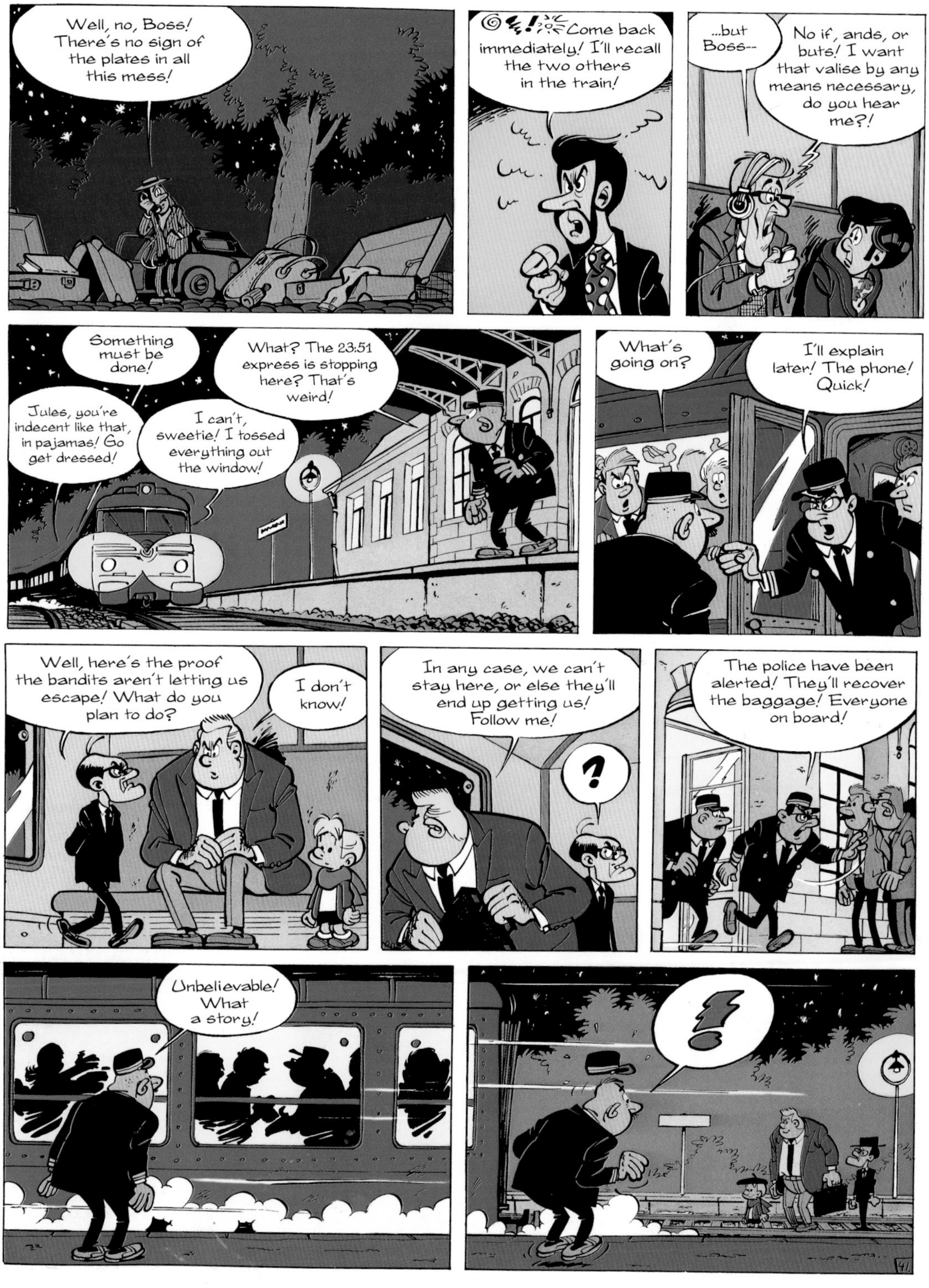
Well, no, Boss! There's no sign of the plates in all this mess!
Come back immediately! I'll recall the two others in the train!
...but Boss--
No if, ands, or buts! I want that valise by any means necessary, do you hear me?!
Something must be done!
Jules, you're indecent like that, in pajamas! Go get dressed!
I can't, sweetie! I tossed everything out the window!
What? The 23:51 express is stopping here? That's weird!
What's going on?
I'll explain later! The phone! Quick!
Well, here's the proof the bandits aren't letting us escape! What do you plan to do?
I don't know!
In any case, we can't stay here, or else they'll end up getting us! Follow me!
?
The police have been alerted! They'll recover the baggage! Everyone on board!
Unbelievable! What a story!
!
41

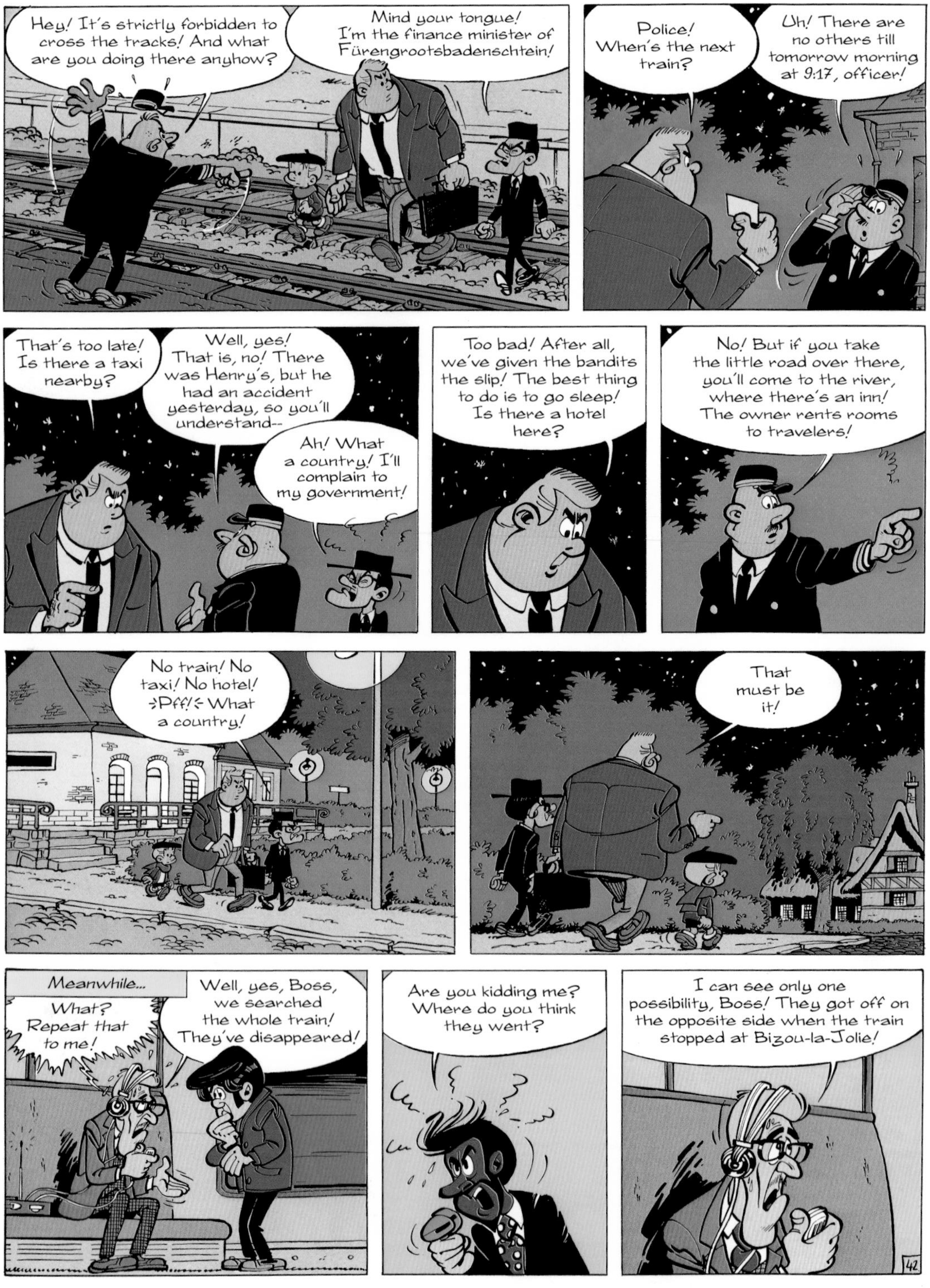
Hey! It's strictly forbidden to cross the tracks! And what are you doing there anyhow?
Mind your tongue! I'm the finance minister of Fürengrootsbadenschtein!
Police! When's the next train?
Uh! There are no others till tomorrow morning at 9:17, officer!
That's too late! Is there a taxi nearby?
Well, yes! That is, no! There was Henry's, but he had an accident yesterday, so you'll understand--
Ah! What a country! I'll complain to my government!
Too bad! After all, we've given the bandits the slip! The best thing to do is to go sleep! Is there a hotel here?
No! But if you take the little road over there, you'll come to the river, where there's an inn! The owner rents rooms to travelers!
No train! No taxi! No hotel! Pff! What a country!
That must be it!
Meanwhile...
What? Repeat that to me!
Well, yes, Boss, we searched the whole train! They've disappeared!
Are you kidding me? Where do you think they went?
I can see only one possibility, Boss! They got off on the opposite side when the train stopped at Bizou-la-Jolie!
42

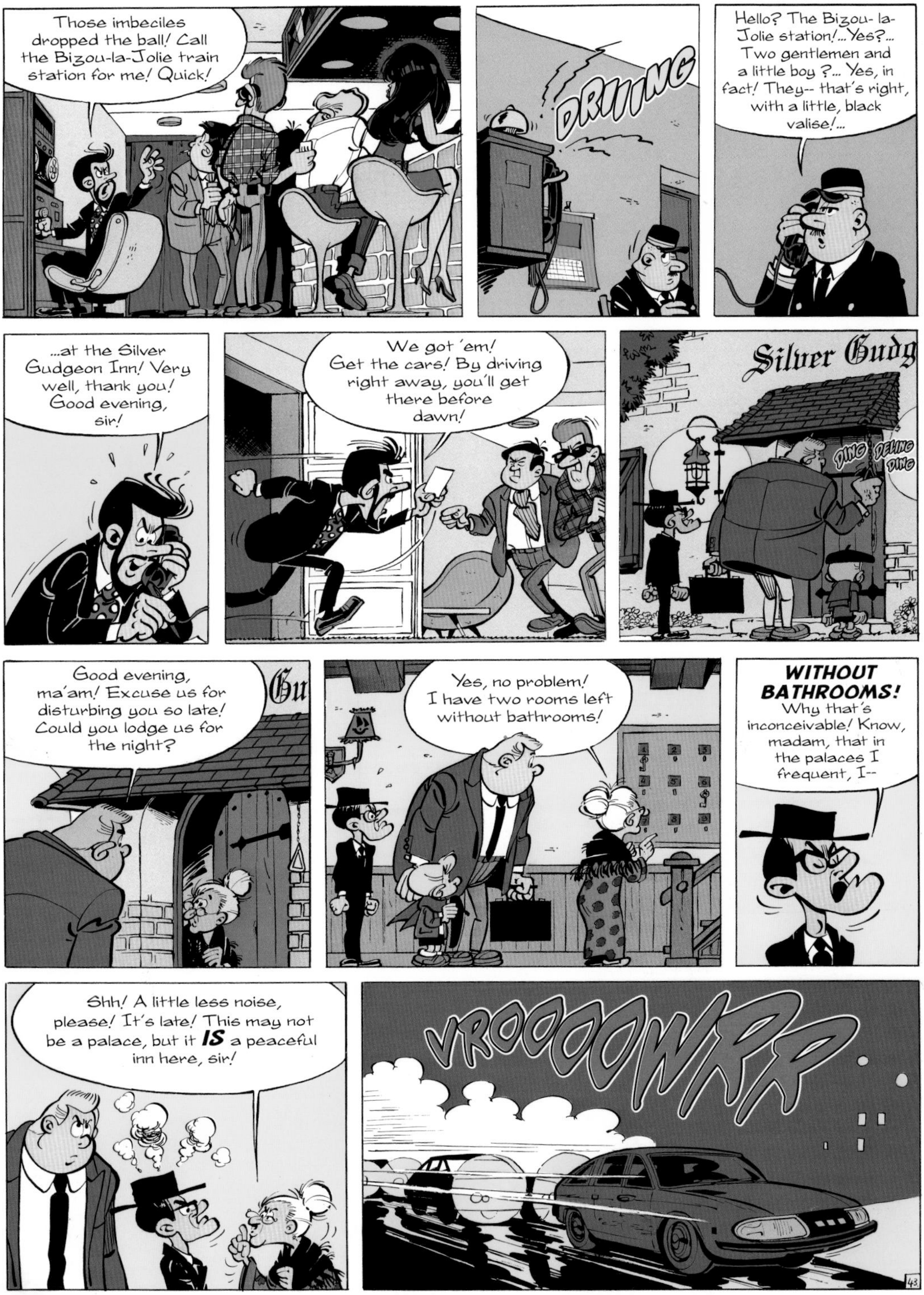
Those imbeciles dropped the ball! Call the Bizou-la-Jolie train station for me! Quick!
DRIIING
Hello? The Bizou- la-Jolie station!... Yes?... Two gentlemen and a little boy ?... Yes, in fact! They-- that's right, with a little, black valise!...
...at the Silver Gudgeon Inn! Very well, thank you! Good evening, sir!
We got 'em! Get the cars! By driving right away, you'll get there before dawn!
Silver Gudg
DING DELING DING
Good evening, ma'am! Excuse us for disturbing you so late! Could you lodge us for the night?
Yes, no problem! I have two rooms left without bathrooms!
WITHOUT BATHROOMS! Why that's inconceivable! Know, madam, that in the palaces I frequent, I--
Shh! A little less noise, please! It's late! This may not be a palace, but it IS a peaceful inn here, sir!
VROOOOWRR
43

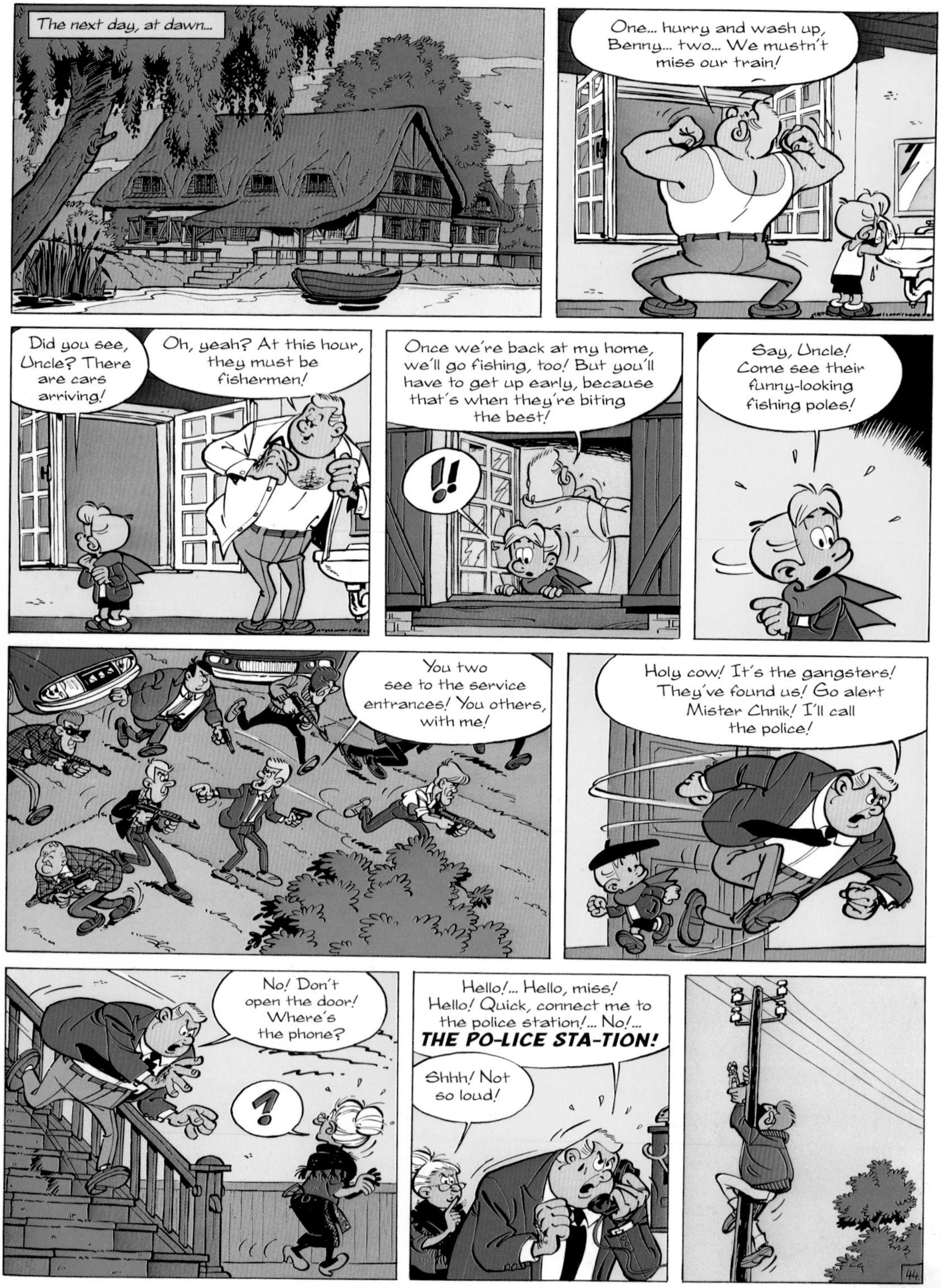

The next day, at dawn...
One... hurry and wash up, Benny... two... We mustn't miss our train!
Did you see, Uncle? There are cars arriving!
Oh, yeah? At this hour, they must be fishermen!
Once we're back at my home, we'll go fishing, too! But you'll have to get up early, because that's when they're biting the best!
!!
Say, Uncle! Come see their funny-looking fishing poles!
You two see to the service entrances! You others, with me!
Holy cow! It's the gangsters! They've found us! Go alert Mister Chnik! I'll call the police!
No! Don't open the door! Where's the phone?
?
Hello!... Hello, miss! Hello! Quick, connect me to the police station!... No!... THE PO-LICE STA-TION!
Shhh! Not so loud!
44

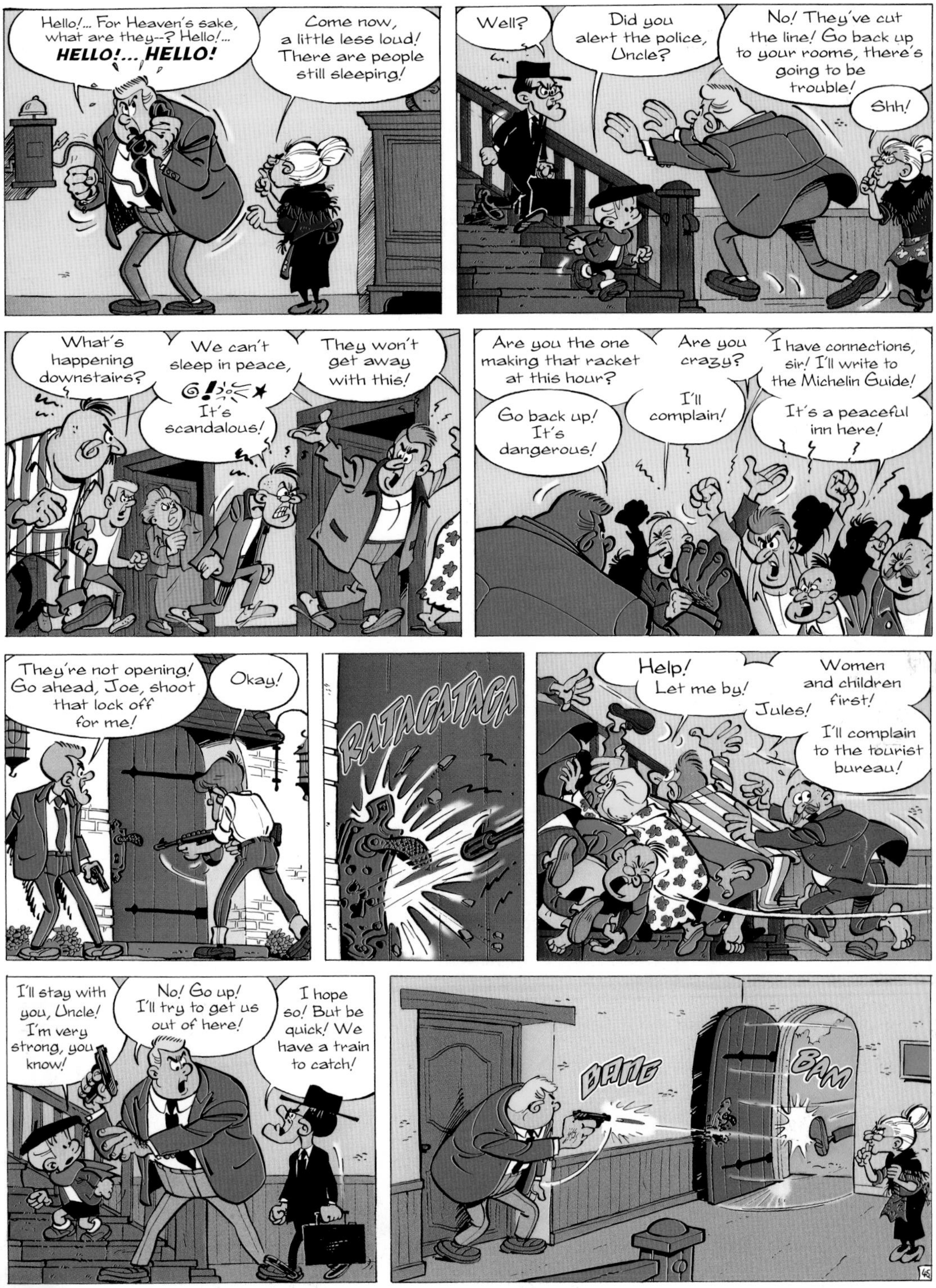

Hello!... For Heaven's sake, what are they--? Hello!... HELLO!... HELLO!
Come now, a little less loud! There are people still sleeping!
Well?
Did you alert the police, Uncle?
No! They've cut the line! Go back up to your rooms, there's going to be trouble!
Shh!
What's happening downstairs?
We can't sleep in peace,
It's scandalous!
They won't get away with this!
Are you the one making that racket at this hour?
Are you crazy?
I have connections, sir! I'll write to the Michelin Guide!
Go back up! It's dangerous!
I'll complain!
It's a peaceful inn here!
They're not opening! Go ahead, Joe, shoot that lock off for me!
Okay!
RATAGATAGA
Help! Let me by!
Jules!
Women and children first!
I'll complain to the tourist bureau!
I'll stay with you, Uncle! I'm very strong, you know!
No! Go up! I'll try to get us out of here!
I hope so! But be quick! We have a train to catch!
BANG
BAM

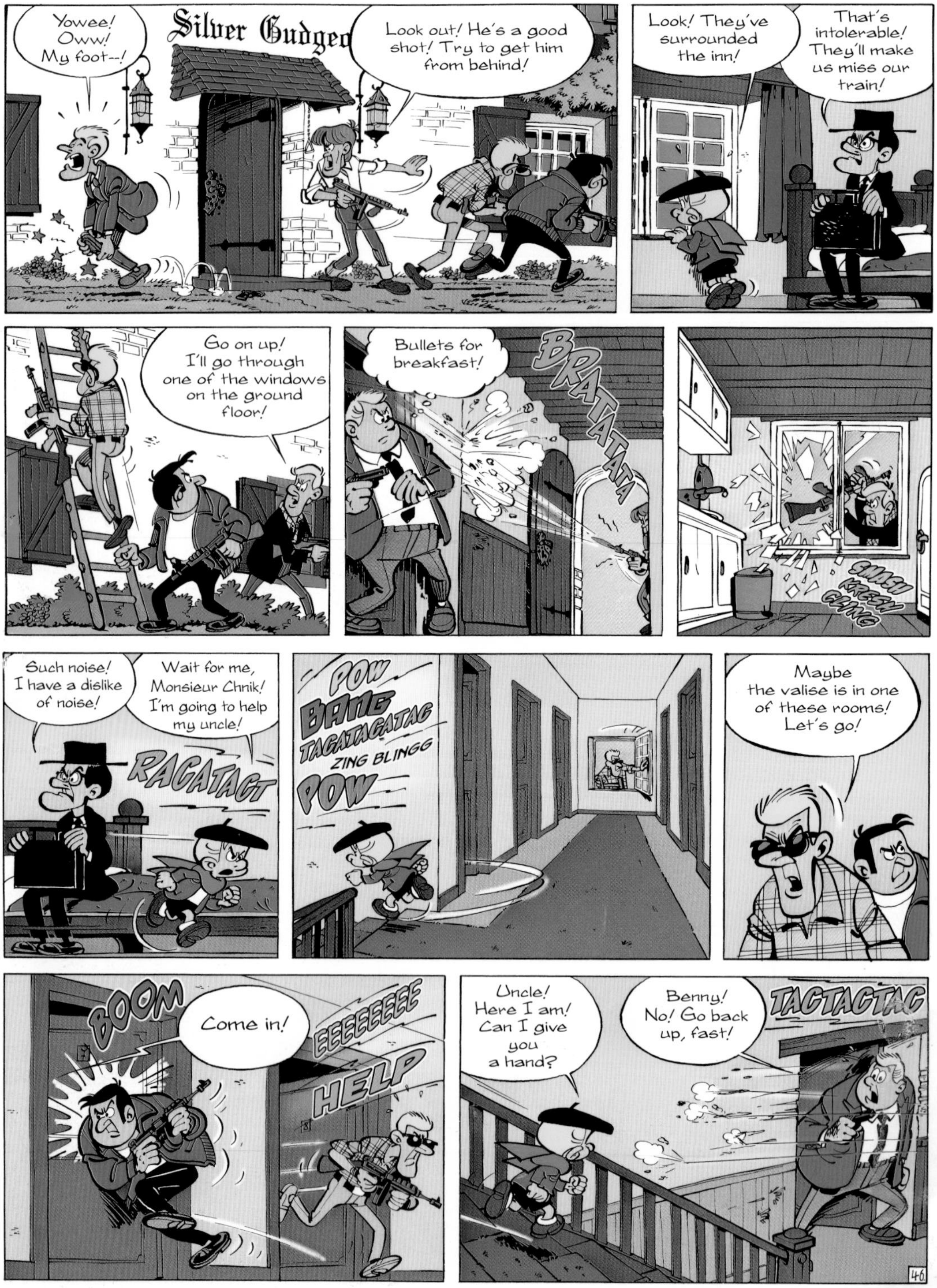
Silver Gudgeo
Yowee! Oww! My foot--!
Look out! He's a good shot! Try to get him from behind!
Look! They've surrounded the inn!
That's intolerable! They'll make us miss our train!
Go on up! I'll go through one of the windows on the ground floor!
Bullets for breakfast!
BRATATATATA
SMASH KRESH CLANG
Such noise! I have a dislike of noise!
Wait for me, Monsieur Chnik! I'm going to help my uncle!
RAGATAGT
POW
BANG
TAGATAGATAG
ZING BLINGG
POW
Maybe the valise is in one of these rooms! Let's go!
BOOM
Come in!
EEEEEEEE
HELP
Uncle! Here I am! Can I give you a hand?
Benny! No! Go back up, fast!
TACTACTAC
46

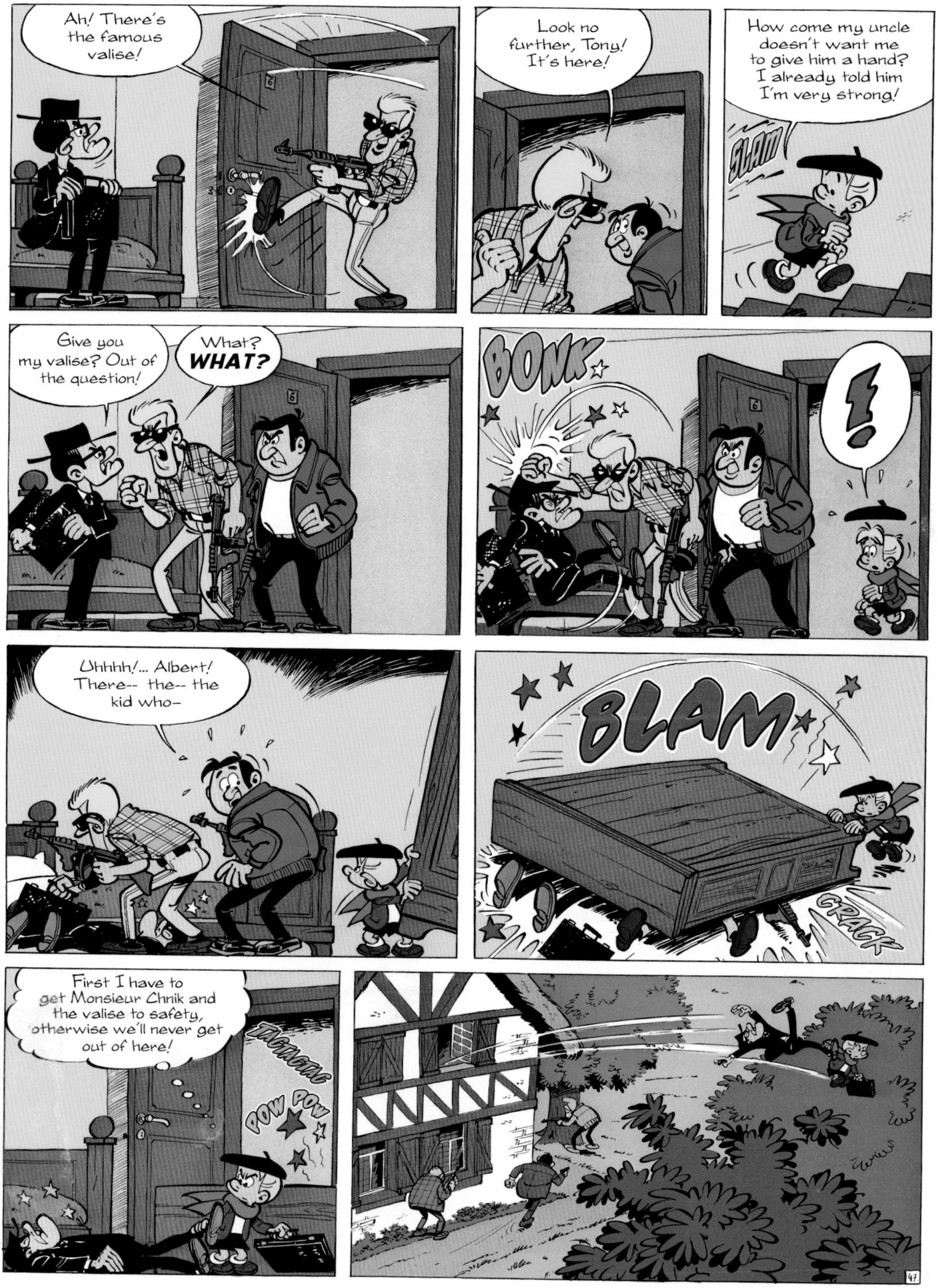

Ah! There's the famous valise!
Look no further, Tony! It's here!
How come my uncle doesn't want me to give him a hand? I already told him I'm very strong!
SLAM
Give you my valise? Out of the question!
What? WHAT?
BONK
!
Uhhhh!... Albert! There-- the-- the kid who-
BLAM
CRACK
First I have to get Monsieur Chnik and the valise to safety, otherwise we'll never get out of here!
TAGTAGTAG
POW POW
47

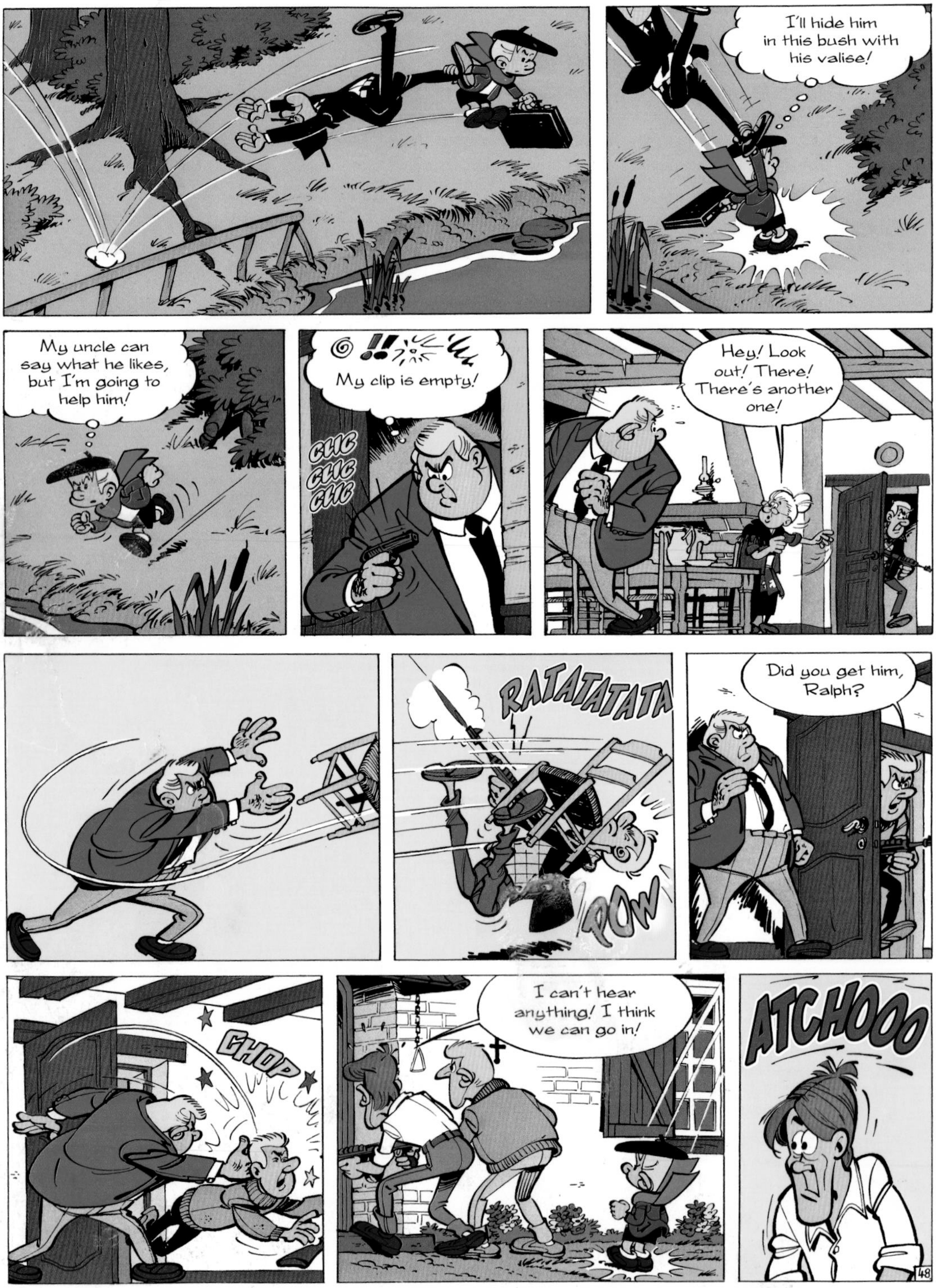
I'll hide him in this bush with his valise!
My uncle can say what he likes, but I'm going to help him!
My clip is empty!
CLIC CLIC CLIC
Hey! Look out! There! There's another one!
RATATATATA
POW
Did you get him, Ralph?
CHOP
I can't hear anything! I think we can go in!
ATCHOOO
48

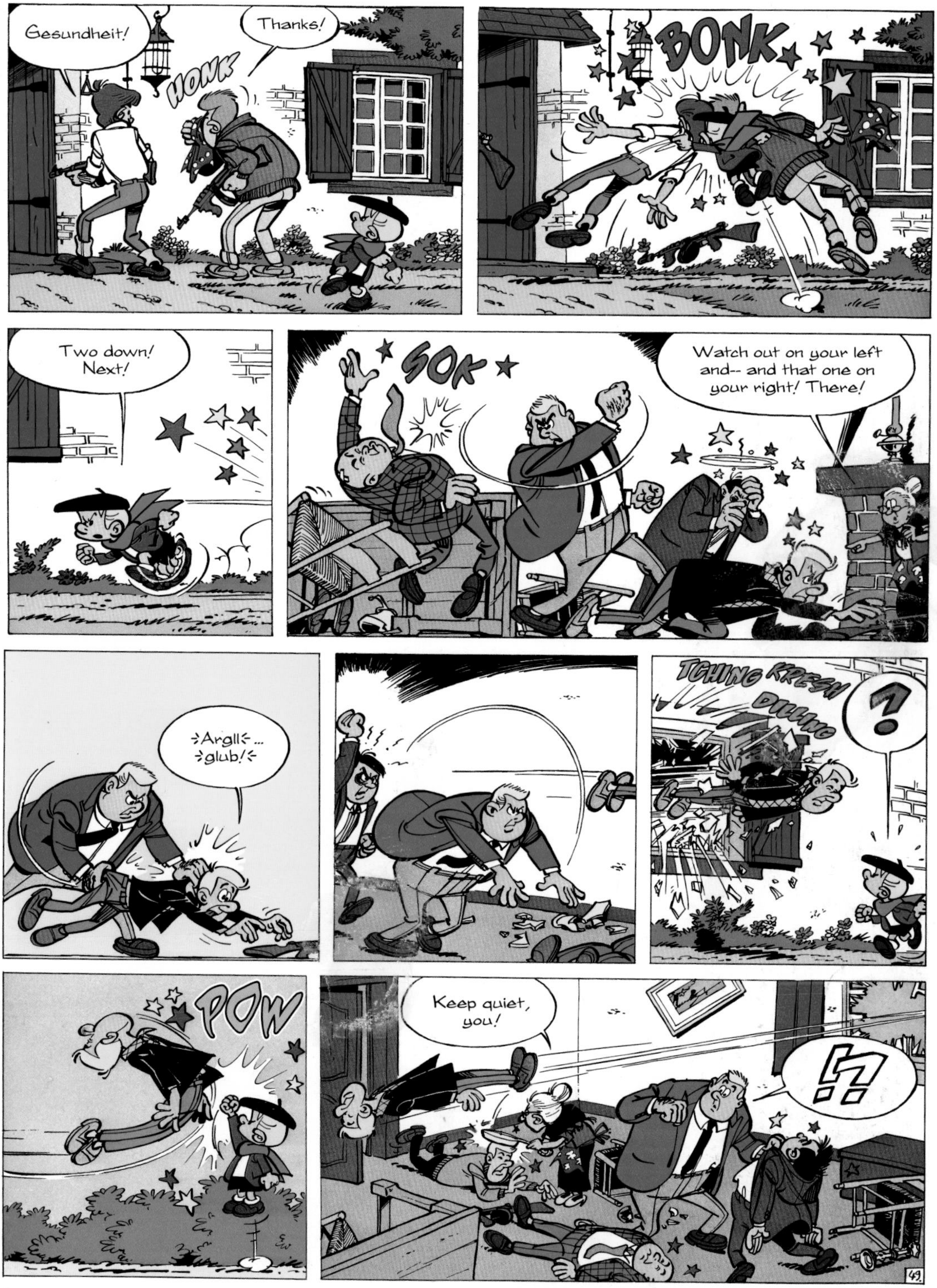
Gesundheit!
HONK
Thanks!
BONK
Two down! Next!
SOK
Watch out on your left and-- and that one on your right! There!
Argll... glub!
TCHING KRESH
DILING
?
POW
Keep quiet, you!
!?

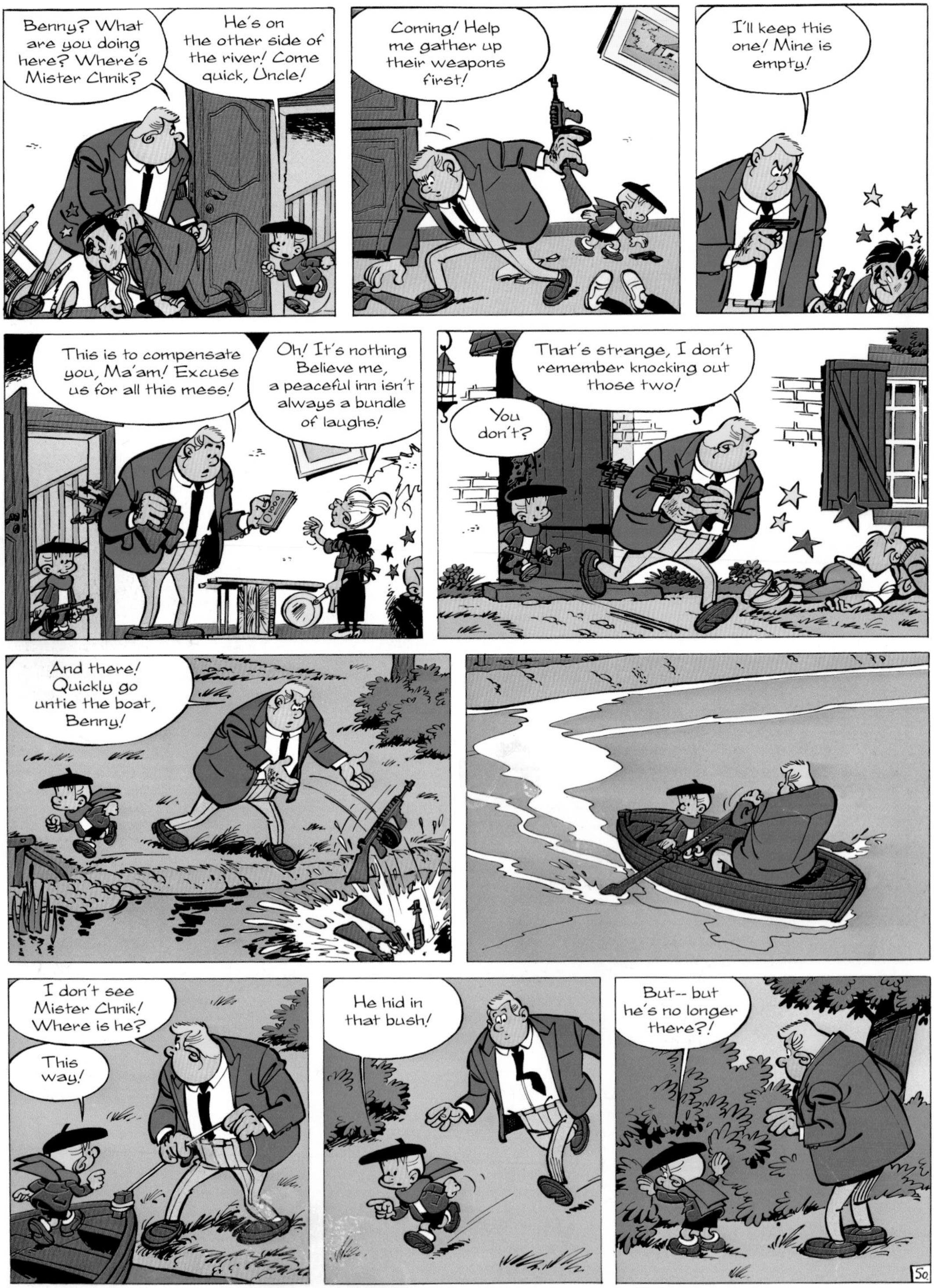
Benny? What are you doing here? Where's Mister Chnik?
He's on the other side of the river! Come quick, Uncle!
Coming! Help me gather up their weapons first!
I'll keep this one! Mine is empty!
This is to compensate you, Ma'am! Excuse us for all this mess!
Oh! It's nothing Believe me, a peaceful inn isn't always a bundle of laughs!
That's strange, I don't remember knocking out those two!
You don't?
And there! Quickly go untie the boat, Benny!
I don't see Mister Chnik! Where is he?
This way!
He hid in that bush!
But-- but he's no longer there?!
50

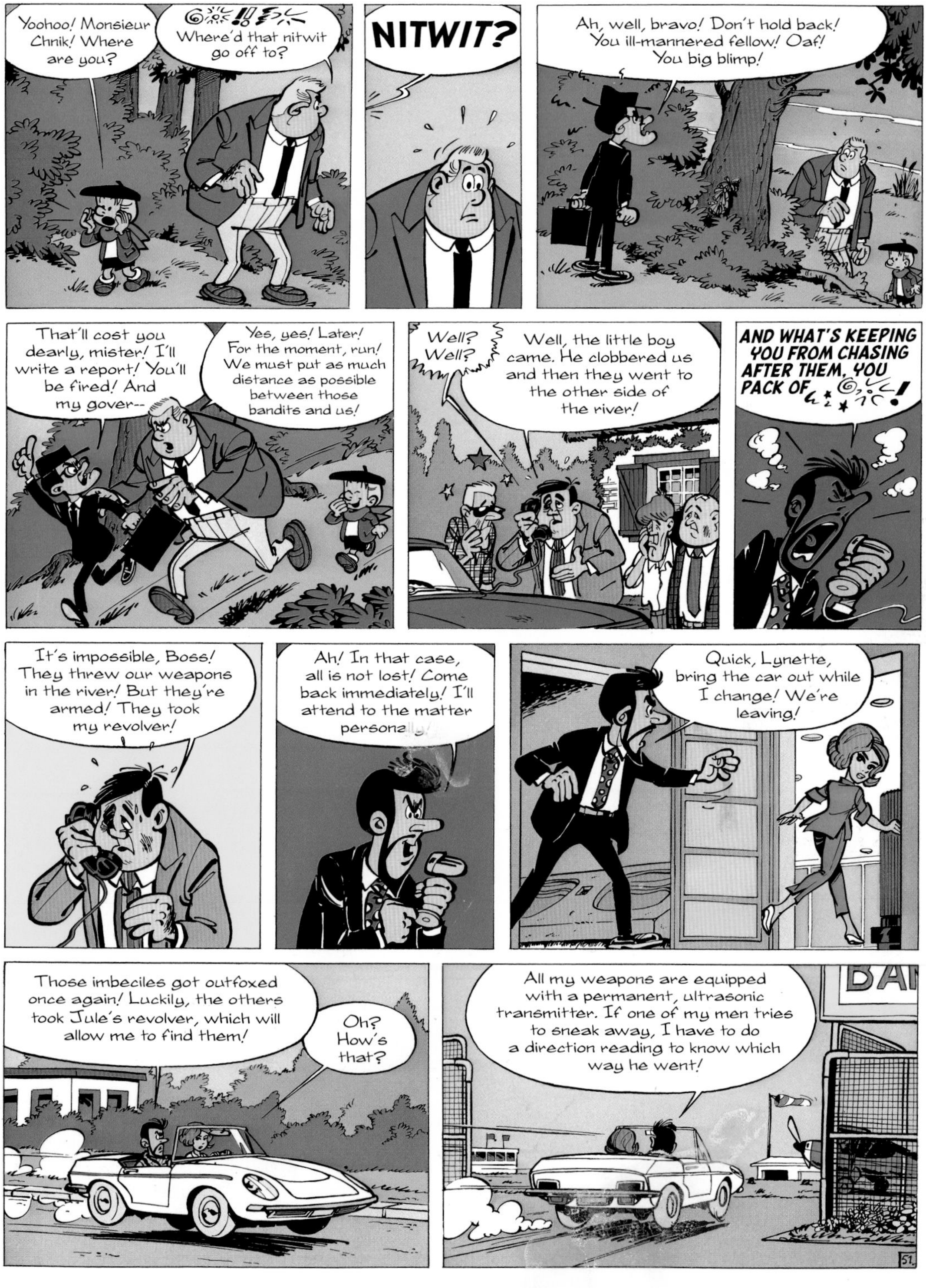

Yoohoo! Monsieur Chnik! Where are you?
Where'd that nitwit go off to?
NITWIT?
Ah, well, bravo! Don't hold back! You ill-mannered fellow! Oaf! You big blimp!
That'll cost you dearly, mister! I'll write a report! You'll be fired! And my gover--
Yes, yes! Later! For the moment, run! We must put as much distance as possible between those bandits and us!
Well? Well?
Well, the little boy came. He clobbered us and then they went to the other side of the river!
AND WHAT'S KEEPING YOU FROM CHASING AFTER THEM, YOU PACK OF
It's impossible, Boss! They threw our weapons in the river! But they're armed! They took my revolver!
Ah! In that case, all is not lost! Come back immediately! I'll attend to the matter personally!
Quick, Lynette, bring the car out while I change! We're leaving!
Those imbeciles got outfoxed once again! Luckily, the others took Jule's revolver, which will allow me to find them!
Oh? How's that?
All my weapons are equipped with a permanent, ultrasonic transmitter. If one of my men tries to sneak away, I have to do a direction reading to know which way he went!
51

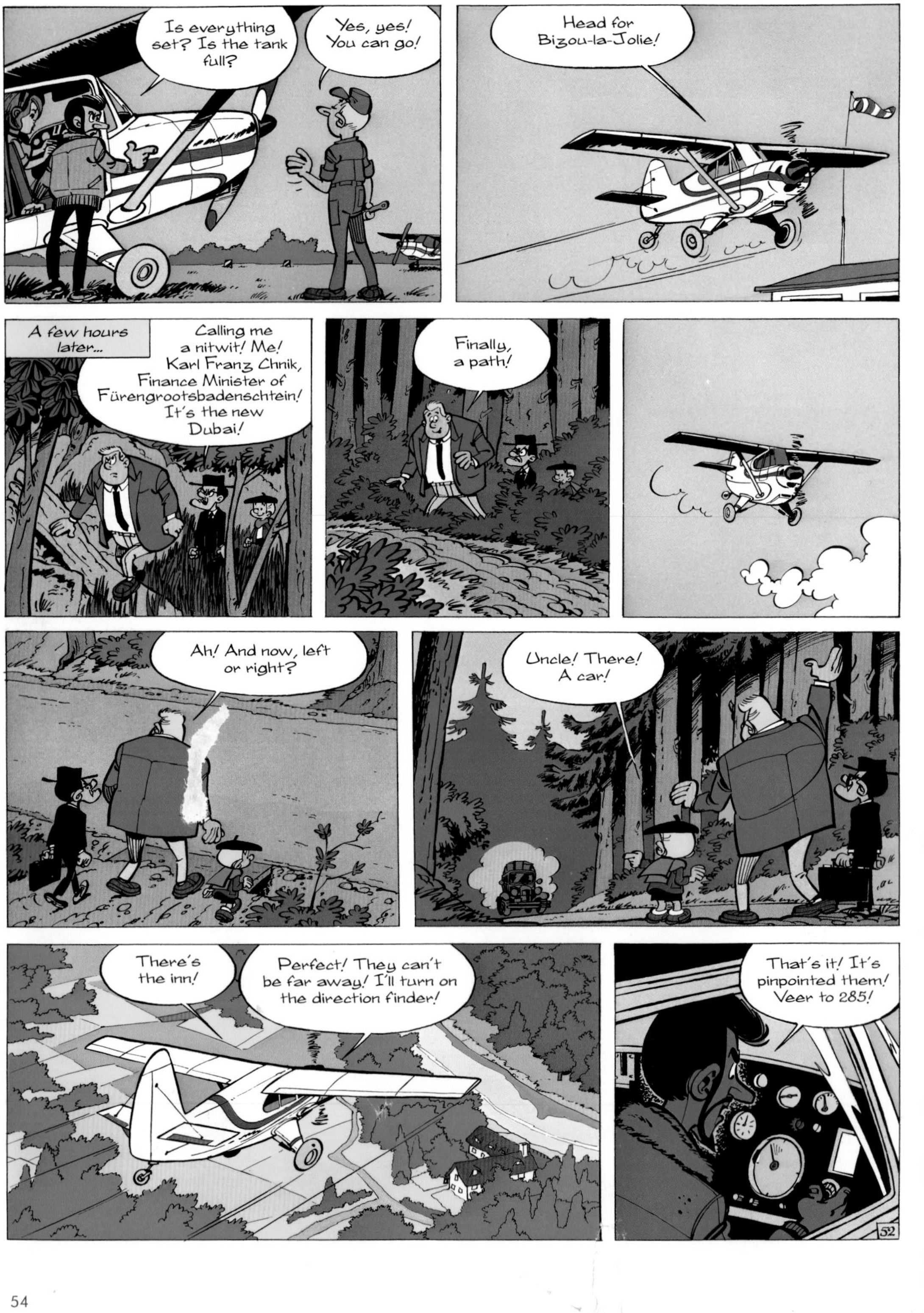
Is everything set? Is the tank full?
Yes, yes! You can go!
Head for Bizou-la-Jolie!
A few hours later...
Calling me a nitwit! Me! Karl Franz Chnik, Finance Minister of Fürengrootsbadenschtein! It's the new Dubai!
Finally, a path!
Ah! And now, left or right?
Uncle! There! A car!
There's the inn!
Perfect! They can't be far away! I'll turn on the direction finder!
That's it! It's pinpointed them! Veer to 285!
52

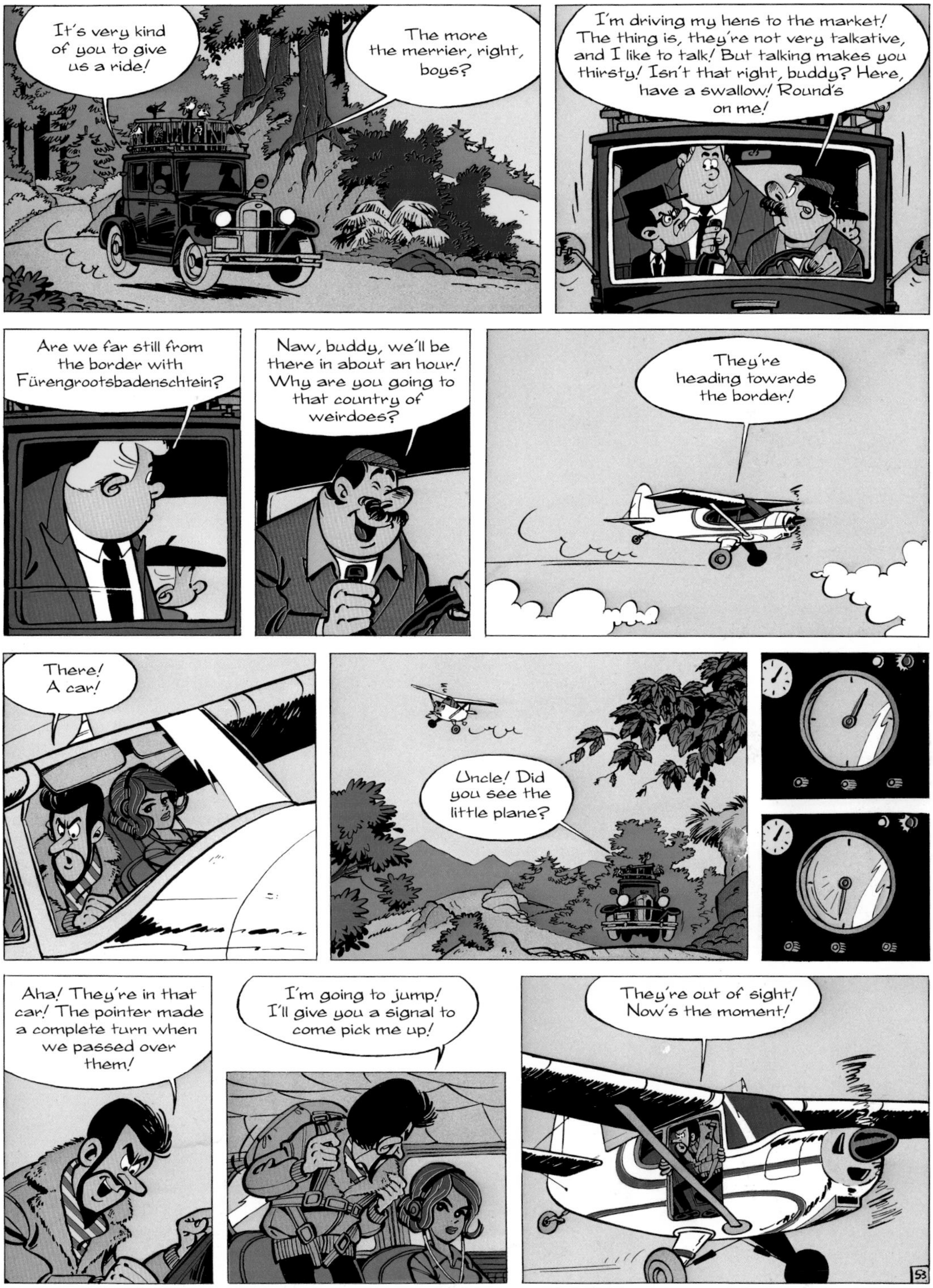
It's very kind of you to give us a ride!
The more the merrier, right, boys?
I'm driving my hens to the market! The thing is, they're not very talkative, and I like to talk! But talking makes you thirsty! Isn't that right, buddy? Here, have a swallow! Round's on me!
Are we far still from the border with Fürengrootsbadenschtein?
Naw, buddy, we'll be there in about an hour! Why are you going to that country of weirdoes?
They're heading towards the border!
There! A car!
Uncle! Did you see the little plane?
Aha! They're in that car! The pointer made a complete turn when we passed over them!
I'm going to jump! I'll give you a signal to come pick me up!
They're out of sight! Now's the moment!
53

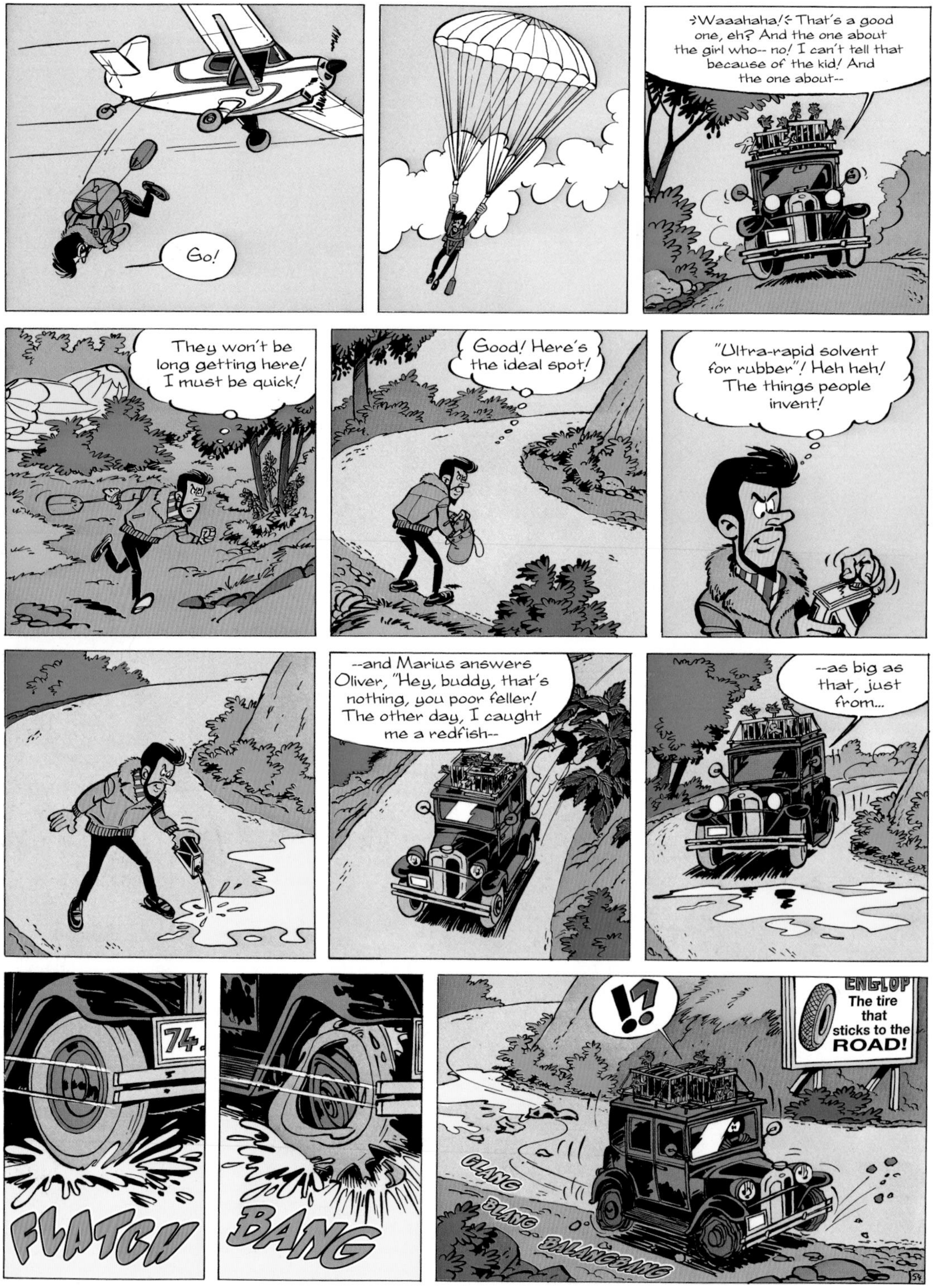
Go!
Waaahaha! That's a good one, eh? And the one about the girl who-- no! I can't tell that because of the kid! And the one about--
They won't be long getting here! I must be quick!
Good! Here's the ideal spot!
"Ultra-rapid solvent for rubber"! Heh heh! The things people invent!
--and Marius answers Oliver, "Hey, buddy, that's nothing, you poor feller! The other day, I caught me a redfish--
--as big as that, just from...
74
FLATCH
BANG
!?
ENGLOP
The tire that sticks to the ROAD!
CLANG
BLANG
BALANGBANG

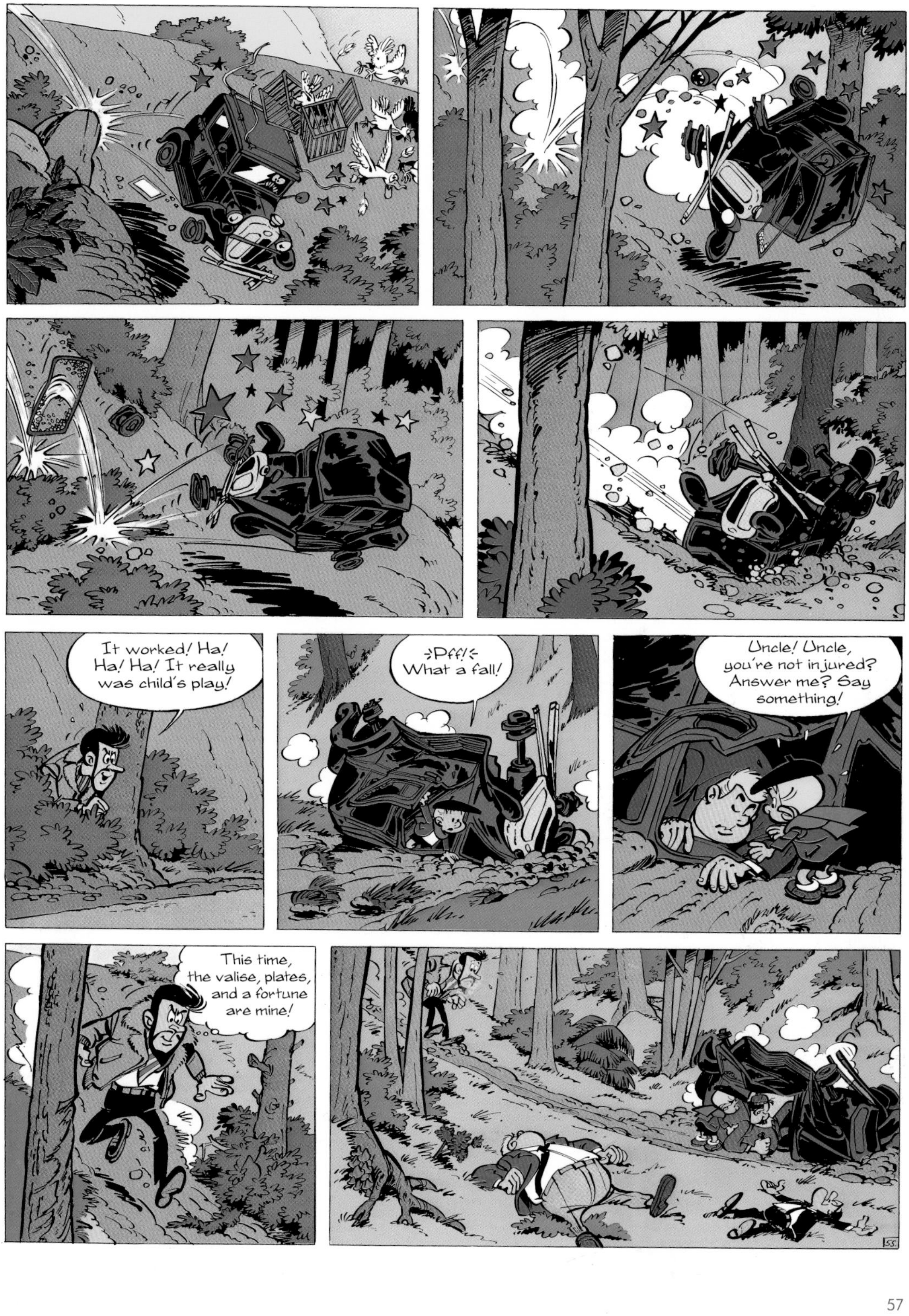
It worked! Ha! Ha! Ha! It really was child's play!
Pff! What a fall!
Uncle! Uncle, you're not injured? Answer me? Say something!
This time, the valise, plates, and a fortune are mine!

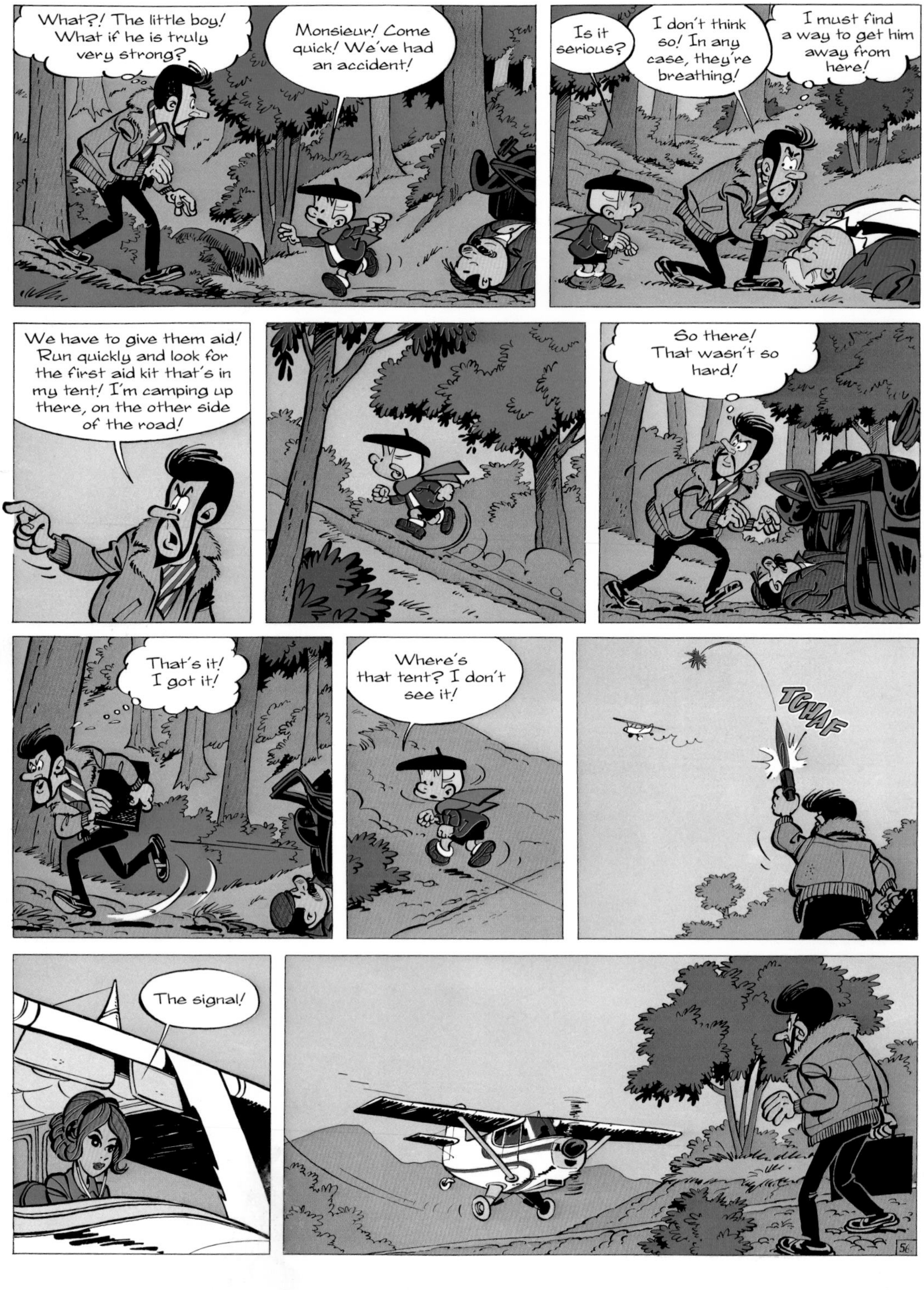
What?! The little boy! What if he is truly very strong?
Monsieur! Come quick! We've had an accident!
Is it serious?
I don't think so! In any case, they're breathing!
I must find a way to get him away from here!
We have to give them aid! Run quickly and look for the first aid kit that's in my tent! I'm camping up there, on the other side of the road!
So there! That wasn't so hard!
That's it! I got it!
Where's that tent? I don't see it!
TCHAF
The signal!
56

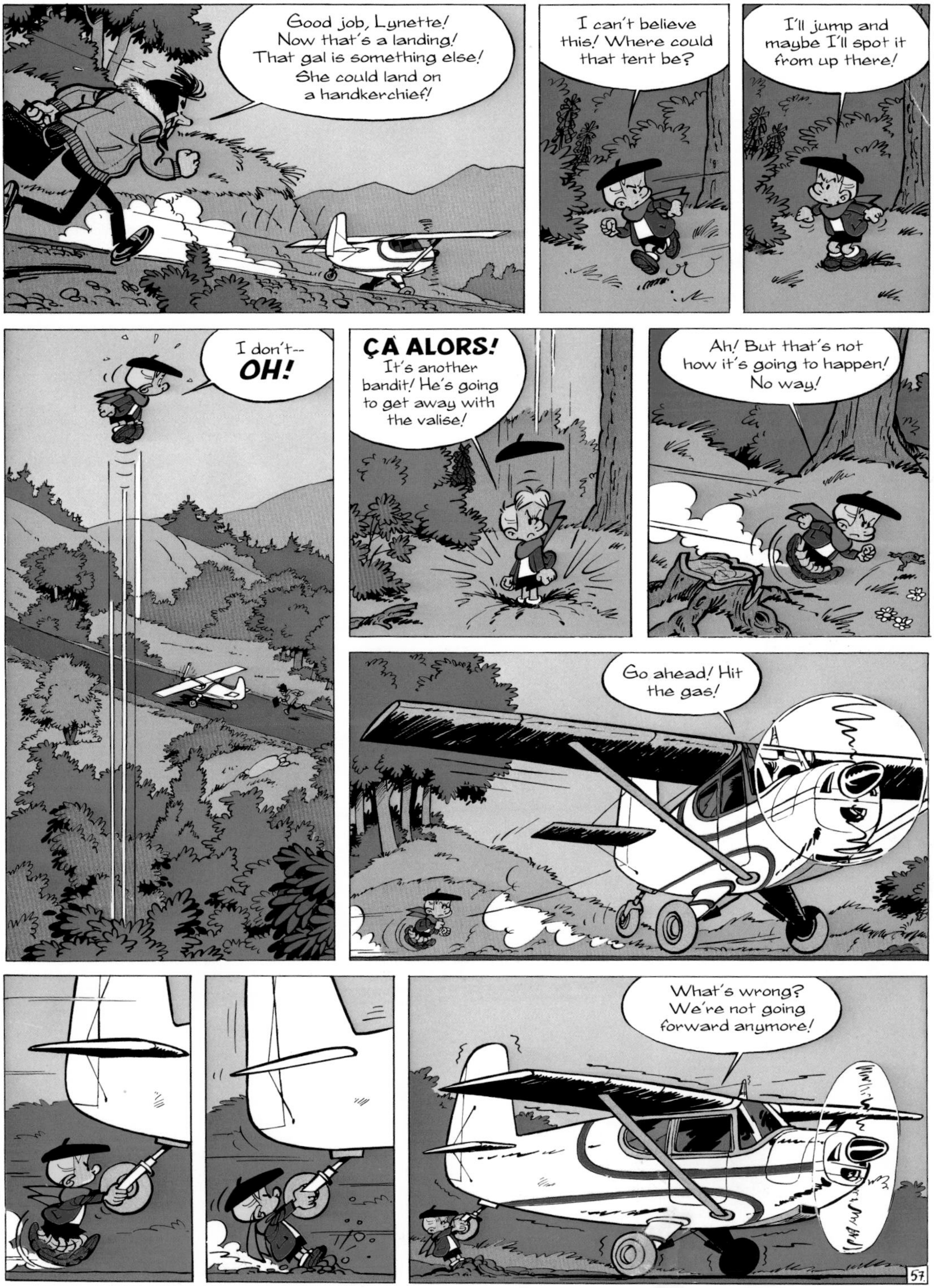
Good job, Lynette! Now that's a landing! That gal is something else! She could land on a handkerchief!
I can't believe this! Where could that tent be?
I'll jump and maybe I'll spot it from up there!
I don't-- OH!
ÇA ALORS! It's another bandit! He's going to get away with the valise!
Ah! But that's not how it's going to happen! No way!
Go ahead! Hit the gas!
What's wrong? We're not going forward anymore!
57.

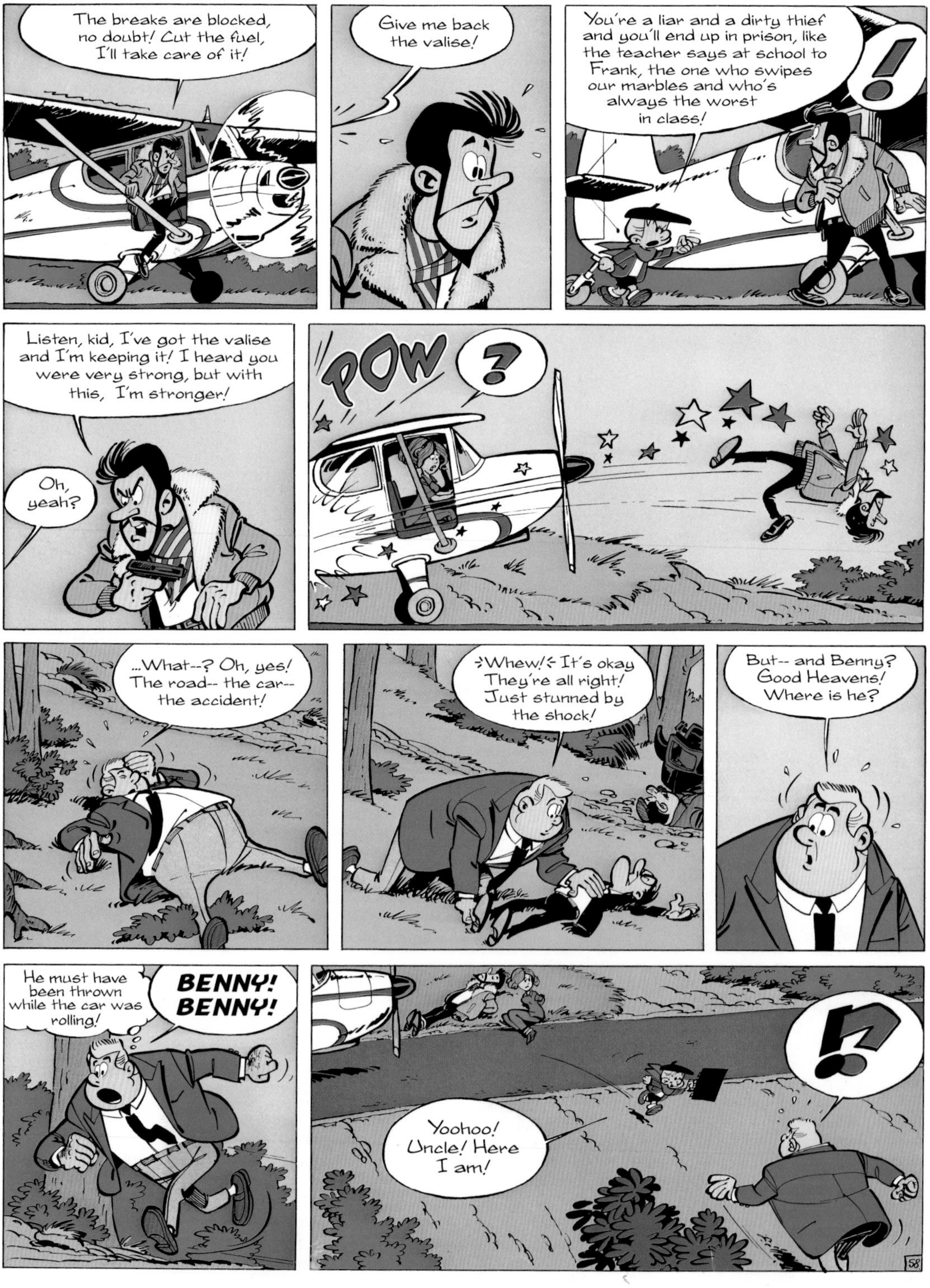
The breaks are blocked, no doubt! Cut the fuel, I'll take care of it!
Give me back the valise!
You're a liar and a dirty thief and you'll end up in prison, like the teacher says at school to Frank, the one who swipes our marbles and who's always the worst in class!
!
Listen, kid, I've got the valise and I'm keeping it! I heard you were very strong, but with this, I'm stronger!
Oh, yeah?
POW
?
...What--? Oh, yes! The road-- the car-- the accident!
Whew! It's okay They're all right! Just stunned by the shock!
But-- and Benny? Good Heavens! Where is he?
He must have been thrown while the car was rolling!
BENNY! BENNY!
?
Yoohoo! Uncle! Here I am!
58

I repeat: we're on Route C.286, at mile marker 23! It's urgent you alert the police! Over!

An hour later...

Be very careful, sergeant, they're extremely dangerous bandits!

Don't you worry!

Okay, buddy, we sure did have a close call, didn't we? Ha! Ha! Ha! That reminds me of the story of the guy who--

By the way, we'll have to remove that plane!

Let me take care of it! Come, Mister Chnik!

You know how to fly, too, Uncle?

Yes! In my career, you have to know how to do everything, Benny!

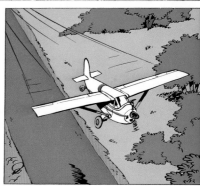

And the one about the guy who didn't know he was condemned to the electric chair? It came as a total shock! Ha! Ha! Ha! Good one, eh?

We just passed the border! Give me the map, Benny!

A few hours later...

Here's the airport! You've finally arrived. Happy, Mister Chnik?

Happy? Ah! Why, no! Not only did you let me get intoxicated at the bank, you almost cost me my life on the highway! Then you drag me around for hours on an ATV that ends up exploding! You abandon me at the airport! You make me buy two valises in order to throw them out the window! I get pummeled in an inn without a bathroom! You call me a nitwit! You put me onto a jalopy driven by a drunkard! And you want me to be happy?

But-- but what are you doing? Are you crazy?

Open the door, Benny!

61

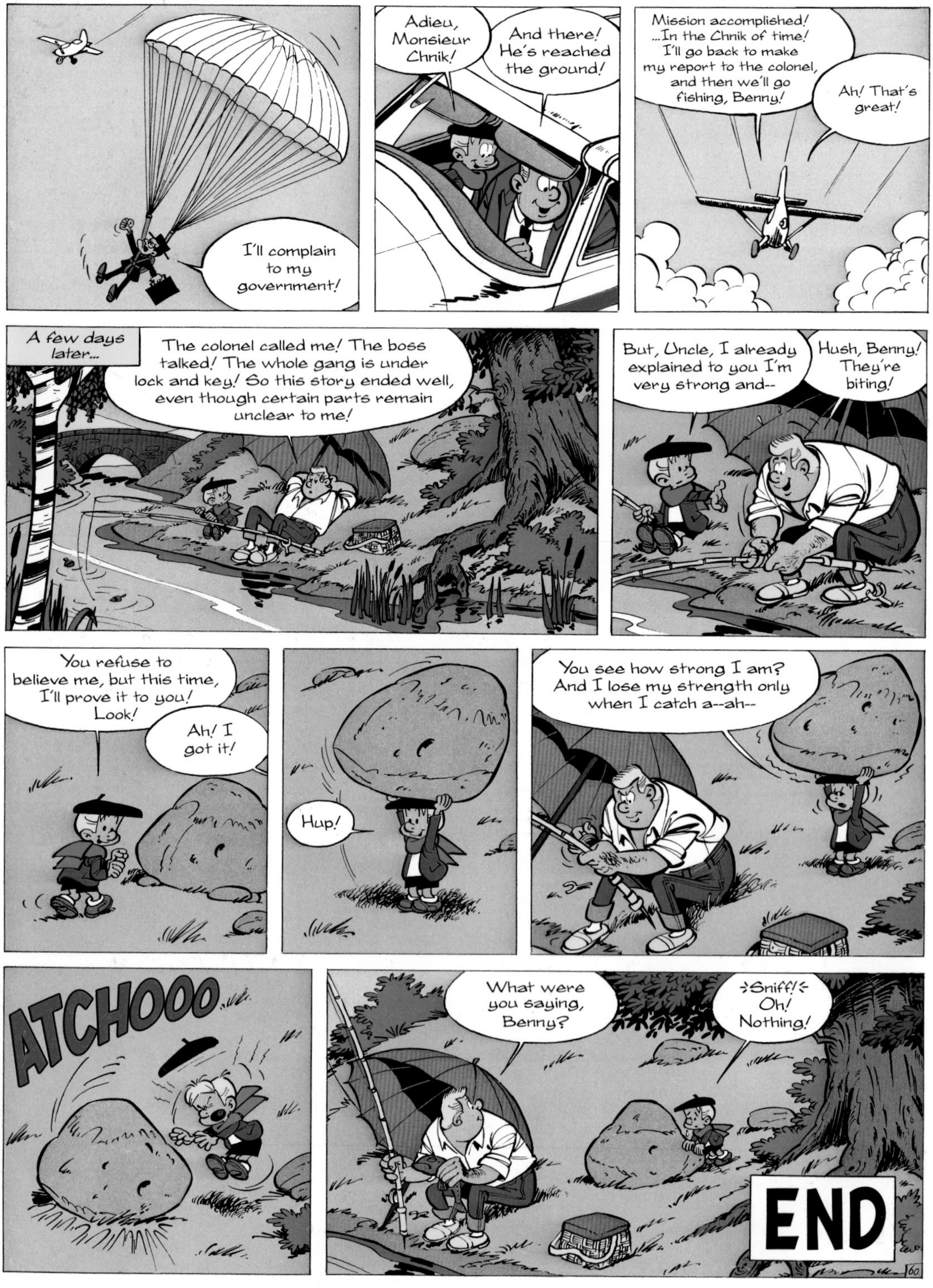
I'll complain to my government!
Adieu, Monsieur Chnik!
And there! He's reached the ground!
Mission accomplished! ...In the Chnik of time! I'll go back to make my report to the colonel, and then we'll go fishing, Benny!
Ah! That's great!
A few days later...
The colonel called me! The boss talked! The whole gang is under lock and key! So this story ended well, even though certain parts remain unclear to me!
But, Uncle, I already explained to you I'm very strong and--
Hush, Benny! They're biting!
You refuse to believe me, but this time, I'll prove it to you! Look!
Ah! I got it!
Hup!
You see how strong I am? And I lose my strength only when I catch a--ah--
ATCHOOO
What were you saying, Benny?
Sniff! Oh! Nothing!
END
60

WATCH OUT FOR PAPERCUTZ™

Welcome to the fast and furious fourth BENNY BREAKIRON graphic novel, written by Pierre "Peyo" Culliford and Roland "Gos" Goossens and illustrated by Peyo and François Walthéry, from Papercutz. We're the pint-size comics company dedicated to publishing great graphic novels for all ages. And we're so proud to be publishing such wonderful Peyo creations such as THE SMURFS, *Johan and Peewit* (in THE SMURFS ANTHOLOGY), and of course, BENNY BREAKIRON. We're also proud to be publishing all sorts of other great graphic novels too, and you can find out more about those at Papercutz.com.

I'm Jim Salicrup, the Editor-in-Chief and newly-appointed Life Coach for Mr. Chnik. While technically part of my job is assembling BENNY BREAKIRON comics for you, it's something I love so much, that I'd probably do it for free! Just when I thought nothing could possibly be more exciting than BENNY BREAKIRON #3 "The Twelve Trials of Benny Breakiron," along comes BENNY BREAKIRON #4 "Uncle Placid"! It's as if Alfred Hitchcock and Steven Spielberg got together and came up with the storyboards for the most action-packed adventure movie ever filmed! Even though "Uncle Placid" was originally published in 1968, when such things as shoe phones and GPS were the stuff of high-tech spy parodies, such as *Get Smart*, and science fiction, it's as exciting as any action blockbuster being released today. I've heard rumors that a Benny Breakiron movie is in production, and I can only hope they look at "Uncle Placid" for inspiration!

Since I know little of the potential movie, I should instead talk about certain aspects of the Papercutz BENNY BREAKIRON graphic novels. Unlike some other European graphic albums Papercutz translates and publishes, aside from his name (*Benoît Brisefer*, literally Benedict Ironbreaker) we've made no attempt to "Americanize" BENNY BREAKIRON. While the series is clearly set in the 60s—the first three books have been set in 1960, 1963, and 1966 respectively—with very few exceptions, we've also made no attempt to "update" anything. And it's because the tone and feel of these stories so perfectly capture that optimistic positive feeling that was so pervasive during the early 60s. And it would be foolish to try and change how Benny looks—he is the ultimate little French boy with his short pants and black beret. But most importantly, Benny Breakiron, as created by Peyo is pure fun, and we'd be foolish to try and change a thing! And as we said, his adventures are as exciting, if not more so, than anything coming out of Hollywood today! We hope you agree and enjoy travelling back in time to enjoy these comic art classics with us!

STAY IN TOUCH!
EMAIL: Salicrup@papercutz.com
WEB: www.papercutz.com
TWITTER: @papercutzgn
FACEBOOK: PAPERCUTZGRAPHICNOVELS
SNAIL MAIL: Papercutz, 160 Broadway, Suite 700, East Wing, New York, NY 10038

And don't forget, Benny Breakiron will return in BENNY BREAKIRON #5 "Bodoni Circus"!

Merci,

Jim

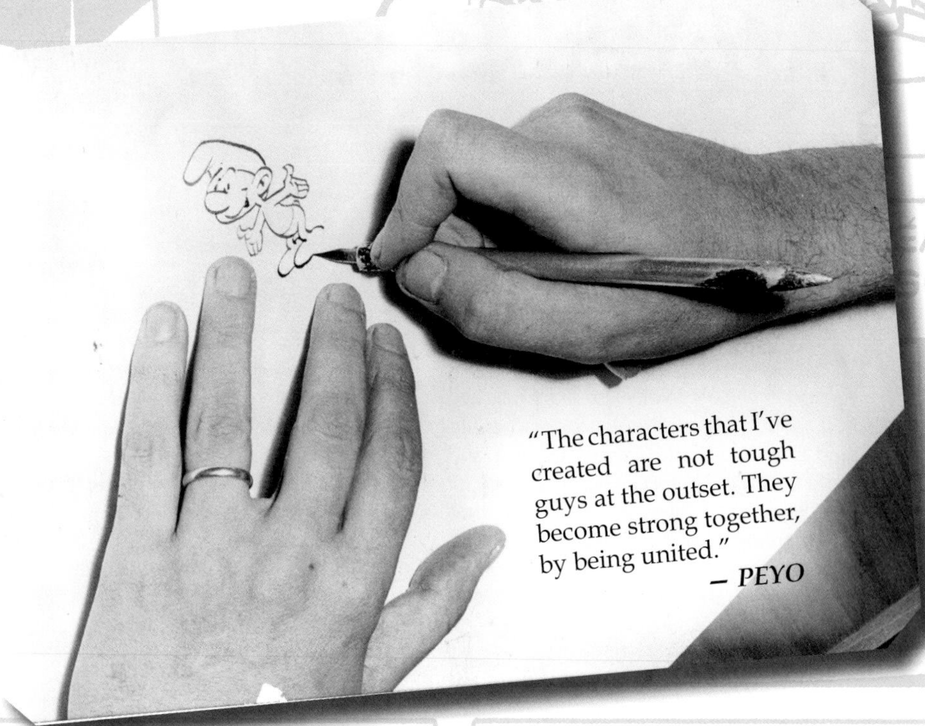
"The characters that I've created are not tough guys at the outset. They become strong together, by being united."
– PEYO

Over 50 years ago, a Belgian cartoonist known as Peyo set his pencil to a blank page and created a worldwide phenomenon we know as The Smurfs. Join us in celebrating more than a half century of humor, camaraderie, heroism, and heart. Experience the master at his best.

The Wonder of Peyo

Incomparable New Graphic Novels From PAPERCUTZ™

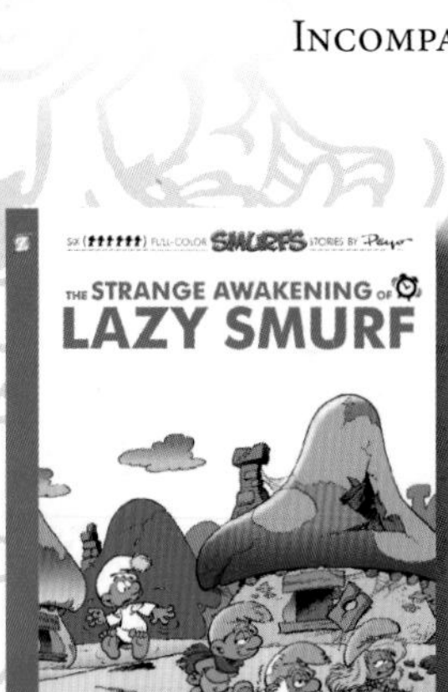
SMURFS STORIES BY Peyo
THE STRANGE AWAKENING OF LAZY SMURF
PAPERCUTZ

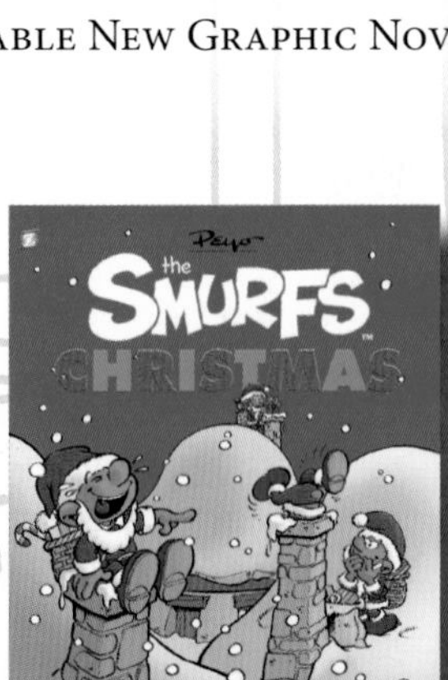
Peyo
the SMURFS CHRISTMAS
PAPERCUTZ

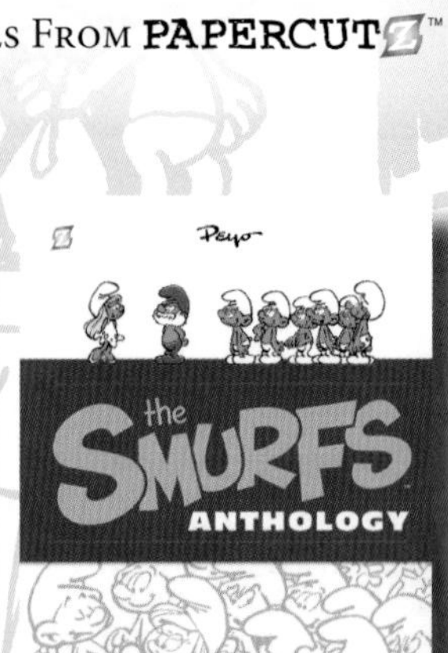
Peyo
the SMURFS ANTHOLOGY
PAPERCUTZ

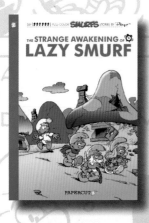

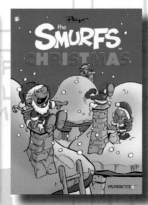

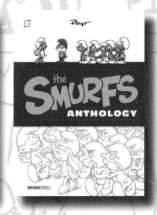

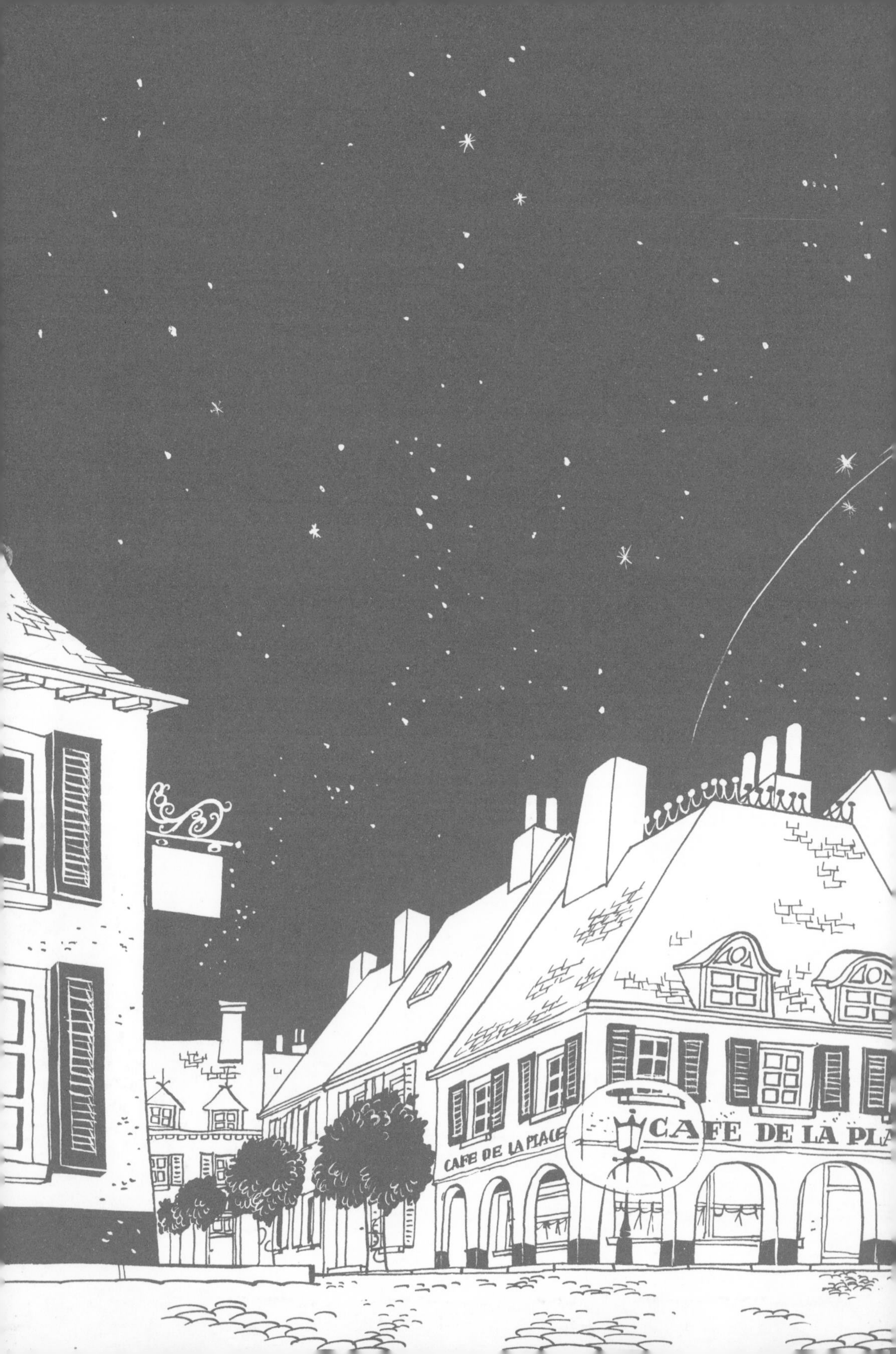
CAFE DE LA PLACE
CAFE DE LA PLA